ask
emma

SHERYL BERK
& CARRIE BERK

YELLOW
JACKET

This is a work of fiction. Any references to historical events, real people, or real places are used fictitiously. Other names, characters, places, and events are products of the author's imagination, and any resemblance to actual events or places or persons, living or dead, is entirely coincidental.

YELLOW JACKET
an imprint of Bonnier Publishing USA

251 Park Avenue South, New York, NY 10010
Copyright © 2018 by Sheryl Berk & Carrie Berk
Yellow Jacket is a trademark of Bonnier Publishing USA, and associated
colophon is a trademark of Bonnier Publishing USA.
Manufactured in the United States of America BVG 1218
First Edition

1 3 5 7 9 10 8 6 4 2

Library of Congress Cataloging-in-Publication Data
is available upon request.
ISBN 978-1-4998-0865-0
yellowjacketbooks.com
bonnierpublishingusa.com

To our friends at No Bully: for all the hard work

you do to make a difference, and your commitment

to lead kids into a cyberbully-free world

CHAPTER 1

DREAMING BIG

"Emma! You're going to be late for school!"

The sound of her mom's bellowing woke Emma Woods out of the most perfect, most amazing dream she'd ever had. In it, Zac Efron was professing his undying love—and posting a selfie with her—on his Instagram feed. It read *#relationshipgoals* and had over a million likes.

"Emma Elizabeth, do you hear me?" her mom called again. "Breakfast is on the table—and it's getting cold."

Emma pulled the covers over her head and willed herself back to sleep. Maybe Zac hadn't drifted too far away. . . .

"Emmaaaaa," her mother called again. "It's seven thirty. The bus will be here in fifteen minutes!"

Emma groaned and crawled out of bed. She knew her mom would never give up. She tossed on a sweatshirt and jeans, brushed her teeth, and swept her blond hair into a messy bun. It was the best she could do given the time limit.

When she finally arrived downstairs at the breakfast table in their kitchen, her older brother, Lucas, had gobbled up most of the pancakes and left her an empty container of OJ.

"You snooze, you lose," he said, snickering while licking the sticky maple syrup off his fingers. "Dad and I helped ourselves to seconds."

"Thirds." Their father looked up briefly from his

newspaper. "Your brother is a growing boy."

"I'm a high school freshman," Luc agreed. "Ninth graders need brain food."

"You need a brain," Emma muttered under her breath. She reached for the only banana left in the fruit basket. "Did you eat the whole bunch? There were six of them yesterday."

Luc tapped his forehead. "Like I said, brain food."

Her mom handed her a granola bar. "This is from my hidden stash," she said, winking. "Luc has no idea where I keep them."

"In the cabinet with the dog's food," he whispered to his sister when their mom's back was turned. Then he sneaked a piece of bacon under the table to Jagger, the family Labradoodle. "There's no pullin' one over on us, is there, boy?"

"You know what your problem is?" Emma huffed. "You think you know *everything*—but you don't."

"I know *your* problem," Luc shot back. "You like to stick your nose where it doesn't belong."

"Do not!" Emma argued.

"Really? What about Harriet's extreme makeover?"

Emma bit her lip. Her BFF had clearly needed a new look for the start of seventh grade this year—it just hadn't gone as well as she'd hoped. "The highlights will fade out . . . eventually," she said.

"What did you do to Harriet?" her father asked, suddenly interested in the conversation.

"She made Harriet look like a skunk with a big white stripe down her head," Luc said, cracking up.

"It was supposed to look like sun-kissed highlights," Emma said, defending her efforts. "I just think we left the dye on too long."

"Ya think?" Luc chuckled again. "Is she still wearing a baseball cap to school every day?"

"I dunno." Emma wrinkled her nose. "Maybe."

"Like I said, you need to mind your own beeswax."

But it was nearly impossible for Emma *not* to step in when a situation needed fixing. Harriet had always hated her mousy brown hair—anything, Emma reasoned, would be an improvement. It wasn't

Emma's fault that her phone battery had died and the timer never went off . . . or was it?

"Five more minutes and she would have been bald," Luc said with a smirk. "Seriously. Emma fried her friend's hair."

"That's enough, Lucas," her mom refereed. "I spoke to Harriet's mom, and they're going to take her to the salon to fix it next week. They just want to let her learn her lesson for a few days."

"But what about her?" Luc said, sticking his pointer finger in his sister's face. "Why doesn't she get grounded? When is she gonna learn her lesson?"

"That is a good question," her mom said. "Em, not everything needs fixing. Harriet was just fine the way she was."

Emma shook her head emphatically. "Uh-uh, she was insecure and miserable. She hated her hair. I was trying to make her feel better about herself."

"I know you were, honey," her mom said. "But sometimes people need to figure things out for themselves."

"Not if I can help it," Emma insisted. "Do you think Dad just sits back and lets people figure things out for themselves?"

Her father raised an eyebrow. "Emma, I'm a cardiologist. It's my job to figure out what's wrong."

"He has a medical degree," Luc piped up. "It's that big plaque on the wall in his office. What's on your wall besides a Justin Bieber poster?"

Emma rolled her eyes. "I'm just saying that if someone asks for my help or advice, I should give it."

"Maybe they should send out an email blast to everyone at Austen Middle School," Luc said. *"Warning! Never ask Emma anything."*

Emma suddenly felt a spark of inspiration. In her case, it was never a lightbulb going off over her head. It was more of a tingling in her fingertips, her own spark of creativity telling her she was onto something.

"Thanks for the great idea, Luc," she said, slapping her brother on the back. "I'll take it under serious consideration."

Emma grabbed her banana and granola bar and headed for the front door. This was one morning she just couldn't be late.

THE WRITE STUFF

Emma raced down the hallway and spotted her two best friends waiting for her at her locker.

Izzy, Harriet, and Emma had met at recess on their first day of kindergarten. They were in line on the school's playground, waiting their turns for the swing set, when Harriet burst into tears because it was taking so long. Izzy and Emma both stepped back, letting her go before them, and the rest was history: instant besties! They were an unlikely trio with not a lot in common: Izzy was a gymnast, a girl who liked the feeling of tumbling and being upside down. Harriet, on the other hand, always had her nose buried in a book and freaked when anything in her life changed even in the slightest. Emma remembered how she cried for a week the previous June when the orthodontist took off her braces! Most girls couldn't wait for that day to come, but Harriet "had gotten used to them." She actually worried that she'd feel like a different person without metal on her teeth.

Then there was Emma. She liked to think of herself as the glue that held them all together. She was the problem solver, the mess fixer, the voice of reason whenever a crisis popped up. When Harriet was horribly homesick at sleepaway camp in fourth grade, Emma wrote her a three-page letter, assuring her that everything would be just fine. And when Izzy was heartbroken over earning a bronze medal at her gymnastics meet, Emma planned a BFF sleepover party complete with DIY manis, pedis, and facials to cheer her up.

Together, the three had weathered all of elementary school and now half of middle school. Emma envisioned them rooming together in college and being bridesmaids at one another's weddings. Of course, the wedding cakes would have to have three tiers—vanilla, chocolate, and pistachio—since none of them could agree on which was the best flavor. Emma was smiling at the thought when Izzy waved a cell phone in her face.

"We got your text," she said. "It sounded important." Somehow, Izzy always managed to look perfectly styled and coiffed—never like she'd fallen out of bed like most seventh graders. Her black bob was swept back into a headband, and her royal blue high-top sneakers matched the color of her T-shirt. "What's the big emergency?" she asked.

"I'm going to write an advice blog!" Emma replied, excitedly.

Harriet looked puzzled. "You mean like Dear

Daphne in *Beauty Beat* magazine? I always did want to write to her and ask how to tweeze my brows so they look like Karlie Kloss's."

"Oh! Did you see what Daphne said about whitening your teeth by chewing on parsley?" Izzy piped up. "I always steal some out of the salad bar in the cafeteria. Works like a charm!"

"Um, I guess those could be potential questions," Emma said. "But I was thinking more serious questions—like about relationships and love and stuff."

"Love?" Izzy smirked. "Em, you've never even had a boyfriend!" Izzy, on the other hand, had Ben, who she'd met at sleepaway camp last summer. He lived three hours away and had recently lost his phone, which presented a bit of a problem for their relationship. His parents wouldn't buy him another, so Snapchatting or texting Izzy was out of the question—and the lack of communication put her in a very bad mood.

"I may not have a boyfriend, but that doesn't mean that I'm not observant and practical," Emma insisted. "I notice things that other people don't."

Harriet nodded. "I think she should write about love." She took off her baseball cap, and the white streak in her hair was still an eyesore. "Beauty advice is probably not your thing, Em."

"So you're going to write this blog," Izzy continued. "How do you know anyone will read it? Or even ask questions?"

"Oh, they will. Everyone wants great advice. Besides, you guys can start it off."

"Me? You want me to write about my very personal relationship with my boyfriend?" Izzy gasped in horror. "No way."

"Why don't you ask Emma how you can get Ben to get in touch with you?" Harriet suggested. "What's it been—three weeks now? Are you sure he remembers who you are?"

Izzy gritted her teeth. "That's not nice to say about Ben. You take it back."

"I will not," Harriet said, insulted. "You've said it yourself a million times."

"He's my boyfriend! I can say it. You can't."

"Well, I'm your best friend since kindergarten—so I can," Harriet insisted.

Emma stepped between them. "All right, there's no need to fight. If you've got a disagreement, just ask Emma—that's what I'm going to call my blog!"

"Fine," Harriet huffed. "I'll write a question to *Ask Emma* about how to give my best friend a reality check."

"And I'll ask about how to deal with a friend who's obnoxious and disloyal," Izzy shot back.

Emma hated to see her friends bickering—but this was so great for her blog! Besides, the three always fought like sisters—and over the silliest things. Usually, the disagreements lasted an hour or two—at the very most a day—then they would all make up over an enormous ice cream sundae.

"As soon as I get my blog up and running, you can send in your questions," she instructed them both. "Don't forget the part about Izzy needing a reality check or Harriet being obnoxious. Love it!"

"Fine!" Harriet and Izzy shouted in unison before storming off in separate directions.

#

Emma couldn't wait till her free period to get to the school computer lab. She found her computer science teacher, Mr. Goddard, staring at a screen.

"I'm starting a blog," she said, bursting into the room.

Mr. Goddard looked up, startled. "You don't say? Is this your computer science project for midterms? I haven't even assigned it yet. . . ."

Emma thought for a moment. "Um, sure. Can you help me set it up?"

Mr. Goddard seemed pleased that one of his students was taking such a strong interest in his class. "You'll need a template for starters," he explained, "and a site that hosts it. Then you'll need a title and a picture or two so people can instantly see what it's about. Who do you want to be able to read it?"

Emma smiled. "Let's start with the entire seventh grade."

"Oh," Mr. Goddard said. "Then I suggest your blog should be a tab on the Austen Middle School website. I'm the administrator for the site, so I can help you with that."

He scrolled through the site till he reached the seventh-grade page. "Okay then. What do you want to call this blog?"

"*Ask Emma*," she said proudly. "And the subtitle should be 'Any problem you have, I'm here to help!'" She thought about what image she wanted. "And how about a picture of a laptop screen with the words *Ask Emma* on it?"

With a few more keystrokes, the tab suddenly appeared in the right-hand corner of the screen, next to the lunch menu button—and Mr. Goddard had even created a graphic that was exactly what she had envisioned. "Your fellow seventh graders can enter their student passwords to gain access," he explained. "Do you want them to be able to send you questions?"

"Oh yes!" Emma said. "The more questions, the better. I want everyone to know they can reach out to me with any issues and I'll solve them."

"That's a lot of responsibility," Mr. Goddard

considered. "Why don't we meet once a week and go over the questions you'd like to tackle. I'll create a mailbox so students can send you their questions, and you can choose which ones you want to post."

"Okay," Emma agreed. "Now, how do I get the word out that my blog is open for business?"

"You write your first post, telling everyone what it's about and inviting them to send you questions," Mr. Goddard said. "I'll create a link that we can blast to the seventh grade."

"Awesome!" Emma said, beaming. She couldn't wait to start typing. But Mr. Goddard put his hand over the keyboard.

"Just understand that when you post your opinions on a blog, not everyone will like what you have to say," he warned her. "You should go home and think before you blog."

Emma shrugged. "I can handle it," she told him. "And trust me—everyone is going to love it."

CHAPTER 3

ASK AWAY!

That night, Emma sat on her bed, her legs crisscrossed, with her laptop perched on her knees. She opened a blank document and let the words flow through her fingertips:

HELLO, AUSTEN MIDDLE SCHOOL
SEVENTH GRADERS!

Welcome to my first post on *Ask Emma*. I know so many of you find middle school a really tough place to navigate. (I sure do!) Every day, we're faced with complicated questions and issues, and it can be hard or embarrassing to talk to an adult about them. I mean, who wants to tell your mom that you're crushing on someone or confide in a teacher that you and your bestie had a humongous fight and now aren't speaking? Being this age isn't easy, but we all have to go through it, right?

That's why I decided to write this blog. I want you to be able to come to me with any problems, concerns, or questions you might have. Seriously, you can ask me anything. I promise not to be judgy—I'll just tell you what I think, my honest and heartfelt opinion, and help you try to find a solution or make some changes. You can take my advice or leave it, that's up to you. But at least you know someone cares and is listening and wants to make your life a little easier and happier. I really do. Helping people is kinda my thing.

I'm so excited to hear from you! So ask away! Got a mess? Don't stress. Ask Emma!

She found Mr. Goddard bright and early the next morning and showed him what she'd written.

"It's very sincere," he said. "Good work."

"So we can post it?"

"I don't see why not," he replied. "Once it's live, I'll send out a blast to all seventh graders this afternoon. Let's see what kind of a response you get."

"Oh, I'm sure everyone is going to write in," Emma said. "I think I'll start off answering maybe ten or twelve questions a day. I have homework and choir practice and other stuff I need to do, but I think that's a good amount."

Mr. Goddard looked surprised. "Ten or twelve a day? I was thinking one or two a week would be ample. I know you want an A on your midterm project, but that sounds like a bit much."

"It has nothing to do with my grade," Emma said. "Like I wrote in my post, helping people is my thing."

"And like I said, let's see what the response is," Mr. Goddard assured her. "I don't want you to bite off more than you can chew."

At lunch that day, Emma tapped her fork nervously on the cafeteria table.

"What's with the drum solo?" Izzy asked her.

"It's my blog. It's going up any minute, and I just want to sneak a peek at it."

Harriet shook her head. "You can't go on your phone at lunch. You know the rules. Ms. Bates will freak." She pointed to their principal, who was roaming between tables, looking for offenders.

"It's so unfair," Izzy continued. "The high

schoolers get to use their phones during the day. Why can't the rest of us?"

Emma grabbed a napkin and began scribbling on it. "That's a great question!" she said. "I'll tackle it on my blog."

"So you're gonna be writing down everything we say from now on?" Harriet asked.

Emma laughed. "Not everything—just anything at Austen Middle that needs fixing. Like the no-phone policy."

Izzy held up a french fry and wiggled it in the air. "Well, if you can get them to let us check our phones during the day, I don't care how often you quote me. It's worth it."

At three p.m., when the last-period bell rang, Emma bolted to her locker, nearly knocking over several students and teachers in her path. She pulled out her phone and scrolled down her list of emails and found the one she wanted. *Attention, Austen seventh graders: New advice blog on school site.* Mr. Goddard had included a link, and when she clicked on it, it took her straight to the post she'd written.

"This is so cool!" she squealed. Now all she had to do was sit back and wait for the questions to come pouring in.

That night at the dinner table, she gobbled down her mom's turkey meatloaf in a hurry.

"Glad you liked it, honey," Mrs. Woods said. "You want seconds?"

"Nope. May I be excused?" Emma asked anxiously.

"Got a lot of homework, Em?" her dad asked.

"No, she wants to go check her blog," Luc informed their parents. "I saw her hitting refresh on the page a gazillion times before dinner."

"Blog? What blog?" her mom asked, surprised. "You didn't tell us anything about a blog."

"It's a project for my computer science class," Emma explained, shooting Luc a dirty look. How dare he spy on her—not to mention blab to their parents before she could tell them herself.

But Luc wasn't about to let it drop there. He was never happy till he got her in trouble. Big trouble.

"It's an advice blog. Emma thinks she's an expert." Her brother smirked.

"An expert? On what?" her dad asked.

"Well, on middle school stuff," Emma assured him. "You know, questions about things that kids go through all the time."

"She's going to tell everyone how to live their lives," Luc continued. "Doesn't sound like a very good idea, does it, Mom?"

Mrs. Woods cleared her throat. "Well, Emma, I think it's very noble of you to want to help others. But I'm not sure a thirteen-year-old girl is the best person to be giving advice to other thirteen-year-olds. Don't you think an adult is a better source of information?"

"Which is why Mr. Goddard is going to help me weed through the questions and check all my responses," Emma said. "I've thought of everything, honest. And I posted my first blog entry today."

"You don't say!" her father said. "And what do your classmates think of it?"

Emma sighed. She had no idea what they thought of it because no one had left a single comment or question in the four hours since it went up!

"I'm not sure just yet," she said. "Mr. Goddard said I should answer one or two questions a week, but I was thinking more like a dozen."

"Ha!" Luc exclaimed. "No one is going to pay any attention to your silly little blog. You know why? Because no one wants your advice, Emma."

Emma threw her napkin down on the table. "Oh yeah? Well, we'll see about that!" She ran upstairs to her room, opened her laptop, and checked the blog page yet again.

Nothing. Absolutely nothing. Didn't any kid in the entire seventh grade have a question they were itching to have answered, a dilemma too tough to tackle, a problem too perplexing to solve? She closed the computer and FaceTimed Izzy.

"I think you forget how busy kids are," her friend reminded her. "I mean, I just got home from my gymnastics practice, and I haven't even checked my email once."

Okay, Emma told herself, *everyone is just extremely busy with homework and extracurriculars.*

They weren't ignoring her or, worse, laughing at her blog. They were simply busy being middle school kids doing middle school things. They'd catch on and learn to trust her . . . eventually.

The entire next day at school, Emma couldn't wait till last period to check her phone. When it was finally three twenty, she clicked on the blog page several times, waiting for the comments and questions to appear. "Come on, come on," she scolded her phone, tapping the screen over and over. She shook it in the air, then squeezed it in a choke hold between her palms. She gazed at the screen: still nothing. Not a single, solitary word in the comment field.

"Ugh!" she cried, hurling the phone to the floor.

"What did that poor phone ever do to you?" a voice asked.

It was a boy, someone Emma had never seen before, leaning on the lockers next to hers. He had thick, dark hair that stood at perfect attention—except for a single wayward strand that fell over his left eye. Following her stare, he swept it away, revealing a pair of impossibly deep blue eyes. "I mean, clearly you're having a high-tech tantrum," he teased.

"Huh?" Emma asked, startled. "Oh, the phone. Yeah, just a glitch."

The boy smiled wryly. "If you say so."

If there was one thing Emma didn't like, it was when someone doubted her honesty. She never minced words, and she never lied—unless it was a teeny-tiny fib that was absolutely, positively necessary for the greater good. "If you must know, I started this new blog, and I was hoping all the seventh graders would respond to it."

"Respond how?" the boy asked. "And do you really need their opinion?"

Emma thought for a moment. "Yes . . . and no," she said. "I mean, I want to help people, and you can't help people if they don't share their problems with you in the first place."

"So you like to gossip."

Emma felt her cheeks start to burn. "I didn't say that," she insisted. "I said I want to help."

"Well, you can help me," the boy replied.

Emma's mood suddenly brightened. "I can? Really? How?"

"You can step away from my locker—you're standing right in front of it, and I need my math book." He pointed to the locker just below hers.

"You're new here, aren't you?" Emma asked, shuffling to the left.

"Does it show?" the boy asked, fiddling with the combination lock. "I've been trying to fly under the radar."

"Why would you want to do that?" she asked. "I mean, most kids at Austen Middle belong to something, some club, some group."

"Like the jocks or the brainiacs or the popular clique?" he asked her. "Yeah, none of the above. I'd prefer to be an undefined variable." He held up his math book.

Emma pursed her lips. "Well, that won't last very long here. Trust me, I know Austen Middle. Nobody wants to be, well, nobody."

"I didn't say I was nobody." The boy smirked. He was actually enjoying taunting her!

"Then who are you?"

He opened his pre-algebra textbook and showed her the name scribbled inside: *Jackson Knight*.

"Knight? Is that even a real name? Or is that, like, your stage name?" she teased.

"I've heard it all before: knight in shining armor, knight and day. There's also Batman, the Dark Knight—my personal favorite. My great-grandfather's name was Kniszewski."

"Aha." Emma nodded. "So your family changed it to Knight."

"Apparently," Jackson answered. "My grandpa said no one could spell Kniszewski. I'm not even sure I can."

There was an awkward silence, and Emma twirled a strand of hair around her fingertip. "Yeah, well, I get that. I mean, if my name was something more complicated than Woods, I might change it. I think a five-to-six-letter last name is ideal."

Jackson looked puzzled—he opened his mouth to say something, but Emma cut him off.

"I could introduce you around Austen, help you make friends," she continued. "I'm on the school yearbook committee, founder of the People for Pets club, lead alto in show choir, and a member of the tennis team."

"Thanks for the résumé, but no thanks," Jackson said. "I've got it under control." He closed his locker and stood there, staring at her. Emma stared back. Even though he was a bit mouthy and opinionated, he did have really nice eyes and a dimple in his chin. . . .

"Are you gonna move?" he asked.

"Oh," Emma replied, realizing she was still in his way—this time blocking his exit down the hallway. "Sorry."

"Hope you fix the glitch," he said as she finally stepped aside.

"Glitch?"

"Your phone, remember? The one you were beating up? I'd hate to see how you treat your laptop."

Emma watched him walk away, never once glancing back over his shoulder in her direction.

"Em," Izzy said, tapping her on the shoulder. "You've been standing there mesmerized for five minutes. Whatcha watching?"

"Watching? Nothing," Emma said, picking her phone up. "I was checking my blog, then I got distracted by this new . . ."

"Ooh, did you get lots of questions?" Izzy asked. "Lemme see!"

She peered over Emma's shoulder at the blog on her screen.

"Not one," Emma said, sighing. "I don't think anyone is reading it."

"Really? It says you have one email," Izzy noted.

"It does?" Emma squinted at the screen. "It does! Oh my gosh! I have a reader! I have a reader!" She danced around Izzy excitedly. "Wait," she said, stopping suddenly in her tracks. "Is this you? Did you send me an email?"

"No!" Izzy insisted. "I mean, I know you told me and Harriet to do it, but I had this huge social studies project to do—a diorama of the ancient Greek agora—"

Emma held up her hand. "Wait. You're telling me this is an actual, legitimate *Ask Emma* question posted by an actual seventh grader at Austen?"

Izzy shrugged. "I guess."

Emma took a deep breath. This was a moment she had to take seriously: her very first question on *Ask*

Emma. She clicked on the mailbox and opened the email. *What came first,* it read, *the chicken or the egg?*

Emma's heart sank. It was a joke. A big fat joke.

"Maybe someone out there is really pondering that question," Izzy said, trying to cheer her up. "I mean, don't you ever wonder? Chicken then egg, egg then chicken? It's very confusing."

Just then her mailbox dinged with a second email. This one said, *If a fork was made of gold, would it still be considered silverware?*

"They're making fun of me!" Emma cried.

"We don't know that for sure," Izzy said, trying to calm her. "It could just be naturally curious people who really want to know the answers. You did say ask me *anything*."

"Look at this one!" Emma pointed to a third email that had arrived. *"Why do noses run and feet smell?"*

"Oh, I get it! That's funny," Izzy said, chuckling.

"They think my blog is a joke!"

Emma turned off her phone and shoved it in the pocket of her hoodie. This was not at all the reaction she had expected from her peers. She had poured her heart out in that blog post, and she had expected them to do the same.

"I'm sure you'll get some real questions soon," Izzy said, putting an arm around her friend's shoulder. "I'll even write one if you want. I have lots of things I wanna know. For example, how do I cheer up my BFF who's bummed about her blog?"

Emma rolled her eyes. When she had asked Harriet and Izzy to write in, she didn't think they'd be the only ones. "It's okay," she said. "Maybe I need to give people a few days to figure out what to do."

"Exactly!" Izzy said. "You know how it is when something is new—people don't know what to make of it."

Out of the corner of her eye, Emma spied Jackson wrestling a protein bar out of the vending machine. He was new and he didn't mind one bit if no one could figure him out. In fact, he kind of liked it.

"Fine. I won't check my email for forty-eight hours," Emma vowed. "I'll give *Ask Emma* a chance to catch on."

But Izzy knew her friend better than that. "You're gonna do *nothing* for forty-eight hours?"

"I didn't say *that*," Emma replied. Jackson looked up and caught her staring at him. He winked at her.

"Who's that?" Izzy asked, noticing their interaction.

"I'm not really sure," Emma said, "but I'm going to find out."

THE NEW BOY

When Emma set her mind to something, there was no stopping her—and Jackson Knight had piqued her interest.

She waited for him to arrive the next morning at their lockers. First period started at 8:30 and it was already 8:20, yet there was no sign of him.

Okay, she told herself, *he's not very punctual*—

which means he doesn't particularly care about doing well at Austen. If he did care, he would be sure to get here on time or even a few minutes early.

When he finally meandered by, his backpack casually slung over one shoulder, Emma jumped to attention. "Well, it's about time!"

"Are you the hall police?" he teased. "I didn't hear the first-period bell ring yet."

Emma checked the clock on the wall: 8:22. "You have eight minutes."

"Yeah, I'm an early bird," he bantered back.

"I was thinking—" Emma continued.

"You were thinking about *me*?" Jackson interrupted her. He reminded her of her dog Jagger with his chew toy—he wouldn't stop tugging away at her!

"I was thinking in *general*," Emma insisted. Why was he always twisting her words? "Why don't you join an after-school club? Make some friends? I can give you a bunch of suggestions—like the skateboard society. They're very cool."

"I'm sure," Jackson said. "But I don't want to join

a club, and I don't need help making friends. It's not my first time in New Hope—my family's from here."

"Oh! You have family here." She leaped at the crumb of information he had just shared. Austen was the best middle school in New Hope, Pennsylvania. Maybe he was from Philly? Or Rose Valley . . . or Harrisburg?

"My mom grew up here, but I was born in New York," he said matter-of-factly.

"Oh, like the actual city?" Emma pressed. She'd been to New York a bunch of times over Christmas breaks with her parents to see the Radio City Christmas show and the tree at Rockefeller Center.

"Yup," Jackson assured her. "Skyscrapers and subways and all."

"Well, that's different," Emma said. "From here, I mean."

"You're telling me," Jackson replied.

Then why did he move here? she wondered. Were his parents splitting up? Had there been some horrible, unspeakable tragedy in his family? Did his old school kick him out for bad behavior? He didn't seem the type. Emma's mind raced to all kinds of scandalous possibilities. Who leaves school a few weeks into the new semester and transfers far away? It made no sense—there had to be a good, juicy story behind it.

"So what brings you to Austen Middle?" Emma pushed. "You must have a really interesting reason for transferring here."

"The nosy students," he fired back. "We don't have those in the Big Apple."

"Oh, but I'm sure you do!" Emma said, ignoring the jab. "Did your folks move you out here? Or did something else happen?"

The boy stared at his feet. "It's really nothing worth talking about."

"You can trust me," Emma assured him. "I write an advice blog, remember? Try me. I'm a good listener."

"Why should people ask you for advice?" He actually seemed curious.

"They do. Or they will," Emma said. "They haven't yet. I'm waiting for the questions to start pouring in."

"Aha!" he said. "That's why you were beating up your phone. Advice blog woes."

"I wouldn't call them *woes*," Emma said. She didn't want him to think her blog was a failure—even if it was at the moment. "It's just taking some time for it to catch on."

"Great, let me know when that happens."

"But I can help you—I'm sure it's hard to fit in when you're new."

"What if I don't want to fit in?" he asked her.

"Well, everyone wants to fit in," Emma insisted. "It's like the unwritten law of middle school."

"Well, I don't," Jackson insisted. "And for the record, I don't know how to skateboard. So no club."

"I could teach you!" Emma gave it one last shot. "My brother taught me and I'm actually pretty good. I can even do an ollie."

Jackson raised an eyebrow. "I have no idea what an ollie is. Do I even want to know what an ollie is?"

"It's the awesome trick where you kinda kick the tail of the skateboard downward while you're jumping to make it pop up in the air," she explained.

"Sounds dangerous."

"Not if you practice—I could show you." Emma wasn't quite sure why she was being so pushy. At first she thought it was because she wanted to help a new student fit in, but then she was pretty sure it was Jackson's infuriating resistance. Why did he have to be so stubborn?

"Like I said, no thanks." He touched her elbow, and she felt a strange flutter of butterflies in the pit of her stomach. "Can I be excused now? You're gonna make me late to first period."

Emma glanced at the clock—it was eight thirty and the sound of the bell suddenly echoed through the corridor. Her computer science class was on the second floor, so now she would be the one who was tardy.

"You made me late!" she shouted after him and raced up the two flights of stairs. She settled into her seat seconds before Mr. Goddard called her name for attendance. Luckily Woods started with a *W*!

"Here!" Emma's hand shot up in the nick of time.

Harriet leaned forward in her seat and whispered in Emma's ear: "Was the school bus late again? I hate when that happens."

"No," Emma said. "I was having a conversation with some new kid and I lost track of the time."

"New kid? You mean Jax Knight?"

Emma's jaw fell. How had Harriet managed to meet him? And how was she already calling him a nickname? "Yeah, how do you know him?"

"Oh, he's in my science class," Harriet explained. "Really smart, really funny, knows the periodic table by heart."

Emma sat at her desk, stewing. Maybe Jackson wasn't a man of mystery—maybe he just wanted to be aloof with her.

"Is he nice?" Emma pressed her friend.

"Nice? Yeah, really nice," Harriet said. "He offered to be my lab partner but I said I wanted to work with Marty."

"Marty? Marty Roberts?" Emma gasped. "Harriet,

he's a disaster! He set fire to the science room with his Bunsen burner last semester! And he's such a nerd! Honestly, what are you thinking?"

"The fire was an accident," Harriet insisted. "He didn't know that rubber cement was flammable, and he got a little too close to the burner with his art supplies. And he's not a nerd! Just because he carries a *Star Wars* backpack . . ."

"Harriet, if Marty's your lab partner, you're going to fail science! You got a C last semester. Besides, what will people say if they see you with him?"

"C-plus," Harriet corrected her. "And really?" She seemed very disappointed. "I love how Marty draws pictures of the experiment materials on his lab reports. And how his glasses sometimes dangle off the tip of his nose."

"Harriet, you can do better," Emma insisted.

"But Marty is fine," Harriet said, sighing. "Sometimes I think you just like changing stuff up because you're bored, Em."

"That isn't true!" Emma protested. "I want the

best lab partner for you. I want the best *everything* for you. You're my best friend and you deserve it."

"I don't know. Marty is a really nice guy."

"Harriet, don't you want an A in chem this semester?" Emma asked.

Harriett shrugged. "Yeah, I guess."

"Then leave this to me." Emma waited till their computer class was over, then grabbed her friend to elaborate on her plan.

"I have a solution," she said. "Tell Marty you made a mistake. You already promised Elton you'd be his lab partner. He's in your class, he's smart and cute, and he never sets anything accidentally on fire."

"Elton?" Harriet groaned. "He hates me! In first grade he once called me 'Harriet Scary-et.'"

"He doesn't hate you—that was his way of teasing you because he liked you," Emma said, patting her on the back. "Remember? He shared his Skittles with you on the playground?"

"After they fell on the floor!" Harriet grumped. "Besides, he probably already has a lab partner."

"Which is why I will ask him and make sure he knows you're the best lab partner in the entire class," Emma said. "You don't have a thing to worry about— I'll make sure you're on the winning science fair team this year."

"Really? You'd do that for me?"

Emma beamed. "What are friends for?"

After she dropped Harriet off at study hall, Emma went to find Elton. She spied him at the water fountain, taking a long sip.

"So, Elton," she began, "who's your lab partner in science?"

The water splashed up and slapped him in the face. "Huh?" he said, wiping his eyes with the back of his sleeve. "Why do you wanna know, Emma?"

"Oh, no particular reason," she said slyly. "Just wondering."

"Well, I told the new kid, Jackson Knight, I would work with him—"

"Mistake! Big mistake!" Emma cut him off before he could say another word. She had to convince him that Harriet was the better choice!

"Why is it a mistake?" Elton asked, curious.

"Why? I'll tell you why!" Emma said, frantically wracking her brain for a reason. Then it dawned on her: "I heard the new kid failed science in his old school," she fibbed.

"No way!" Elton gasped. "I had no idea. I got a B-plus last year and I was counting on an A this year!"

"Which is why you need a new lab partner ASAP," Emma insisted. "I'm looking out for you."

"Thanks," Elton said, scratching his head. "I guess I'll have to ask someone else."

"You know, I think Harriet might be looking for a partner," Emma pointed out. "And she just loves science. It's her thing."

Elton nodded. "Really? Okay, good to know."

Emma skipped down the hall, very pleased with herself. She'd made sure Elton was available as a lab partner—now she just had to convince Harriet to send Marty on his way.

"I don't want to hurt his feelings," Harriet said hesitantly when they were at lunch. "I know I said I would dump him as my lab partner, but now I'm not so sure I can. . . ."

"You can and you have to," Emma insisted. "Harriet, have I ever steered you wrong?"

Harriet pointed to her hair. "Highlights?" she reminded her friend.

"Besides that time," Emma replied. "I have a very strong feeling about Elton. Not only is he the perfect lab partner, but he is also perfect boyfriend material."

Harriet took a bite of a chicken nugget and considered. "Boyfriend? You think he could be my boyfriend?"

"Absolutely! And do I have to remind you that Elton came in first place in the science fair last year with his project, 'Suck It Up: The Capillary Action of Plants'?"

"He *is* really smart," Harriet agreed.

"Not to mention captain of the boys' soccer team and very popular," Emma added. "And don't you think he kinda looks like Nick Jonas . . . if you squint your eyes a little?"

"Okay," Harriet finally conceded. "If you really think Elton will be okay with me as his lab partner."

"Okay? He'd be lucky to have you!" Emma said cheerfully. "Didn't you say your lima bean plant grew taller than everyone else's?"

"That was back in third-grade science," Harriet reminded her. "This is seventh grade. We don't do lima beans anymore."

"Even so," Emma said, "this is a perfect partnership on all counts. Trust me."

She got up from the table and found Elton in line for the mac and cheese with mini meatballs.

"So, it's all set, then," she said, sneaking up behind him. Elton jumped again, this time almost dropping his plate.

"What's set?" he asked. "And how come you always pop out of nowhere?"

"Your new lab partner," Emma reminded him.

"Uh, I'm not sure," he said, helping himself to a

heap of elbow noodles. "I think I'll just stick with Jax."

"Elton, we discussed this," she said gently. "Remember I told you to ditch him?"

"You told him to ditch me—why?" a voice asked behind her.

Emma gulped. While she had been sneaking up on Elton, someone else was sneaking up on her.

"Oh, wait! Let me guess: it's because you heard I failed science in my old school," Jackson piped up. "Which is an absolute, one-hundred-percent lie. I got an A-minus. You need to check your gossip sources next time you try and spread a rumor." He walked off, annoyed.

Emma felt awful. Not only had she been caught telling a little white lie, but she now had to apologize to Elton, Harriet, *and* Jackson for trying to play musical lab partners.

She'd meant well—Harriet really needed someone better than Marty to help raise her grade, not to mention her social status. Elton would have been a great choice if Jackson hadn't gotten involved. But that was just it—he was always there, everywhere she looked, buzzing in her ear like an annoying little mosquito! But he had seemed genuinely hurt that she would gossip about him behind his back. She hadn't meant to—it was just the only way to get Elton to pair up with Harriet!

"Um, so I'm not ditching Jax now, I guess," Elton said sheepishly.

Emma nodded. "Yeah. I must have been misinformed. Sorry about that."

Harriet waved at her from across the cafeteria. Now Emma had to tell her friend she'd failed her too.

"It turns out Elton wasn't a good choice," she began. "My bad. You can stick with Marty."

"What? I can't. I just told Marty that I had to switch partners because I was afraid of my hair catching on fire. So now I have no lab partner? Emma, what did you do?"

"Just tell him you changed your mind," Emma coached her. "Or you were delusional from hunger and made an itsy-bitsy mistake."

Harriet buried her head in her hands. "It's like the highlights all over again!" she cried. "Em, I know you mean well, but you keep ruining my life!"

Emma had never meant to make such a mess! She heard her brother's voice echoing in her ears: *When are you going to learn your lesson?* Now not only was Harriet furious, but who knew what Jackson was saying about her. He was probably telling everyone right now that she was a liar—wasn't that what he had called her to her face? She didn't even know Jackson well, yet surprisingly, what he thought about her mattered. She didn't want him to think she was just a silly mean girl who went around gossiping. She wanted him to understand that she hadn't meant to hurt his feelings; she just wanted to help Harriet. But if she tried to tell him any of the above, chances were he'd just storm off again. So she decided there was only one way to right things. She went to the computer lab and began typing:

Dear Emma,

I told a lie about someone and now he probably hates my guts. I don't know how I can ever make things right. Help!

Sincerely,

Sorry I Said It

Then she took a deep breath and wrote an answer—the very advice she would give anyone in this situation, including herself:

Dear Sorry,

Lies never lead to anything good—even if your reason behind them is helping a friend. So here's what I think you should do: Set the record straight. Don't just tell him you're sorry, make sure everyone else knows the truth so you put an end to any rumors. For example, let's just say you told a lie about someone failing a class in his old school when he actually got an A–. You should do your very best to make sure people know that was his real grade. And in the future, don't talk about people behind their backs for any reason. You can hurt someone and you might not be able to undo the damage. Hope that helps and he forgives you for fibbing!

XO,

Emma

She sent the post to Mr. Goddard, asking him to post it ASAP. Then she crossed her fingers and hoped Jackson would eventually see it and know how sorry she was. What if he didn't read it?

She was always saying she could fix anyone's problems—but now she wasn't sure if she could even fix her own.

5 STICKS AND STONES

The next morning when Emma got to school, she saw Mr. Goddard coming out of the teachers' lounge with a mug of coffee.

"Did you get my post?" she asked him anxiously.

"I did, and I put it up early this morning," her teacher told her. "That was quite a tough question that reader sent in. I think you gave her sound advice."

"It's up? Already?" Emma felt the room spinning. That meant Jackson might have seen it!

"You said ASAP," Mr. Goddard reminded her.

"I know, but I didn't think it would be as ASAP as in this morning!"

She ran to her locker and pulled out her phone to check. After her answer, there was a single, anonymous comment—written in bold, all-capital letters:

YOU WANT MY ADVICE? STOP WRITING THIS STUPID BLOG! YOU STINK!

Emma felt like someone had punched her in the stomach. Mr. Goddard had warned her that people might not agree with her opinions, but he never said someone might attack her so personally! Who would do such a thing?

"We saw, Em," Harriet said when she and Izzy finally found her huddled in a corner windowsill in the girls' bathroom. They had been searching for her all morning. "I'm so sorry. You don't stink."

Emma shrugged. "Maybe I do."

Izzy sniffed the air. "Nope, you smell like the vanilla perfume I gave you for Christmas."

Harriet hugged Emma. "You meant well—you always do. I talked to Marty and we're back on as lab partners, so we're all good."

"It's not good. I'm shutting down my blog," Emma vowed. "It's done. Over."

"Em, you can't!" Izzy pleaded with her. "You're just getting started! There are kids out there who need your help."

"Yeah, like who?" Emma sniffled.

"Like me," Harriet said. "So now that Marty is my partner again, how do I get him to ask me out?"

"Don't ask me," Emma said. "I'm the last person you want to ask for advice." Tears stung the corners of her eyes.

"But I did ask," Harriet said. "I wrote a letter to *Ask Emma* this morning. I expect an answer right away. Before Marty asks someone else!"

"I wrote one too," Izzy said. "I want to know how to get Ben to tell me how he really feels about me."

"That's really nice of you both, and I appreciate it, but you don't need me to fix your problems. Whenever I try to, I just make a bigger mess of everything."

"'Got a mess? Don't stress.'" Izzy quoted her friend's very first blog post. "Someone really smart once said that. Wonder who it could be?"

"Guys, no one likes what I have to say—that comment someone posted made that perfectly clear."

"So some big mouth didn't like it—that's his or her problem, not yours," Izzy insisted.

"At least talk to Mr. Goddard before you quit," Harriet suggested. "I'm sure he'll have good advice for your advice blog."

"Fine," Emma said, drying her tears. "I'll talk to him."

Mr. Goddard read the comment over several times, then took off his glasses. "We will delete it immediately," he said. "I'm appalled that one of your fellow students could be so rude."

"I guess I just don't understand why," Emma said. "I mean, why would someone write that?"

"For many reasons," Mr. Goddard said thoughtfully. "Sometimes, out of anger, jealousy, frustration. Other times, to try to look cool in the eyes of peers. Sometimes, just to get a reaction out of you."

Emma looked at the screen and winced. "What would you do if you were me?" Emma asked him.

"I can't answer that for you," her teacher replied. "We talked about how starting a blog would open you up to criticism. It comes with the territory. Someone once said of the great novelist Jane Austen—whom our school is named for—her writing is 'without genius, wit, or knowledge of the world.' And we all know that isn't true."

"Wow, that's harsh," Emma said.

"It was, but it was also just someone's opinion. Do you think you have something important to say, Emma?"

Emma considered for a moment. "I do. I have a lot to say. I haven't even really gotten started yet."

"Then don't let anyone silence you," Mr. Goddard

said. "I think we can take some measures and restrict your fellow students from commenting on your posts," Mr. Goddard said.

Emma shook her head. "No, that's not what a real blogger does. It should never be one-sided. Students should be able to comment."

"Not if those comments are hurtful and uncalled-for," Mr. Goddard said.

"Like you said, everyone is entitled to an opinion," Emma said. "Maybe some people don't like what I'm writing—I guess that's okay. I can always delete. But at least I know one thing—people are reading it."

"They are," Mr. Goddard said. "*Ask Emma* is gaining an audience."

She saw both Harriet's and Izzy's letters waiting for her in her inbox. "I'd like to post another blog entry tomorrow," Emma said. "ASAP."

Mr. Goddard smiled. "You truly mean ASAP . . . or should I wait for you to think about it first?"

"No," Emma said. "The sooner the better." She was afraid she might change her mind.

When she left the computer lab, she walked straight into Jackson, who was waiting for his social studies class to begin next door. In all her hysteria over the mean comment, she'd almost forgotten the real reason she'd written the post—to apologize to him!

"Hey," he said, noticing her.

"You're speaking to me?" she asked, looking around to make sure he wasn't greeting someone else.

"Yeah, I guess."

Emma blushed. "I wasn't sure—I mean, you were pretty mad at lunch yesterday."

Jackson shrugged. "That's ancient history. Roman, actually—I have a quiz on Julius Caesar."

Oh, good! He was changing the subject. "He was murdered," Emma recalled from a term paper she'd written on the Roman emperor. "His friends conspired against him." Then she thought about the cruel comment again and it made her sick to her stomach—what if the whole seventh grade was now conspiring against *her*?

Jackson read her mind. "Harriet filled me in during science," he said. "I'm not one to gossip, but I heard someone wrote some negative stuff on your blog."

Emma was now officially mortified! Was everyone talking about it? Had Jackson seen what was written about her and agreed with it?

"For the record, you shouldn't care what people think," he told her. "I mean, so what? Some people think I failed science in my old school, and I could care less." He smiled.

"I'm sorry about that," she said. "Really, truly sorry."

"So I read. What kind of advice columnist answers her own problems?"

"Please," Emma begged. "Not you too. I can't take anymore people criticizing me or my blog today."

"Well, maybe you'll get some more letters from real people with real problems," he suggested. "If I have any problems, I'll be sure to send them your way."

"You sure you don't have any?" Emma teased back. "New kid, no friends . . ."

"No friends? What about us?"

Emma's heart suddenly skipped a beat. "Oh, yeah. Sure," she stammered.

"See, problem solved! Good job, *Ask Emma.*" He strolled into his classroom, leaving her behind to ponder what had just happened. Was he saying he actually liked her and considered her a friend? Suddenly, the events of the morning faded into the background. Jackson was right: Who cared what people thought about her? As long as *he* thought about her . . .

When she got home from school that day, Emma wanted to go straight upstairs and start typing away on her laptop. She took off her coat, dropped her backpack on the couch, and went to the fridge for a glass of milk. Luc was already home, seated at the kitchen counter with a bag of chips in front of him.

"What? No 'Hi, big bro. How was your day?'" he asked her.

"Hi, big bro. My day started out pretty awful."

She sat down next to him and dug into the bag. "Then it got a little better."

"Ah, middle school. I remember those days like they were yesterday. . . . " Luc said.

"They *were* yesterday. You're only a freshman in high school," Emma reminded him. She took a bite of a jalapeño-flavored chip and spat it out. "With really bad taste in after-school snacks!"

"You gotta dip it," he said, passing her a container of guacamole. Emma wrinkled her nose but tried it. Surprisingly, it wasn't half bad.

"You see? I do know my snack foods," he bragged. "And I also know what happened today at Austen. I have spies everywhere."

By spies he meant Elton, whose big brother was one of Luc's best friends.

"Someone dissed your blog, huh?" Luc said.

"I don't wanna talk about it," Emma replied, stuffing another chip into her mouth. The last thing she wanted now was for Luc to say "told ya so" and make her feel even worse.

"Okay, I'll talk and you can listen," he said. "Don't pay any attention to what those idiots have to say.

They're just losers with nothing better to do than pick on someone trying to do something good for other people."

Emma stared. Was Luc sticking up for her? Defending her? This was a first! "You mean that?" she asked him.

"Well, yeah," Luc said. "I don't say stuff I don't mean. And neither do you. I read your blog, and it was actually pretty good."

Emma smiled, then remembered something. "Wait, you read it? How? You don't have an Austen Middle School student account anymore."

"Oh, I know," Luc said, chuckling to himself. "I just used yours."

Emma's eyes grew wide. "What? You know my student password?"

"Please," Luc said, grinning. "You underestimate my talents. I know all your passwords. I even know where you keep the tiny little key that unlocks the diary in your nightstand."

"Luc!" Emma screamed, punching him in the arm. "That is not any of your business!"

"Well, I guess minding other people's business

runs in the family," he teased her. "Fine, I won't sign in on the Austen portal as Emma Woods anymore. But if you ever wanted to show me your posts . . . well, I'd be cool with reading them."

Emma took the glass of chocolate milk Luc had poured himself and stood up. "I'll be in my room writing my next post if Mom and Dad get home and are looking for me," she said.

"I got it. Do not disturb. Blogger at work."

She started to walk upstairs but stopped to tell her brother one last thing. "Luc?" she called down to the kitchen.

"Yeah?"

Emma smiled to herself. "Thanks."

Emma opened her laptop and clicked on the first email. She recognized the question as Harriet's:

Dear Emma,

How do I get a boy in my class to pay attention to me?

Sincerely,

Never Been Noticed

The question was a good one, and Emma was beginning to ponder it herself. Jackson certainly liked to tease and torment her, but did he really see her as anything more than a friend? She began to type.

Dear Never,

Obviously, if you're standing right in front of him, he sees you—the question is how does he see you? As just some random girl in his homeroom—or as potential girlfriend material? You can't read minds—but you can read signals. Does he always start a conversation with you? Does he take the empty seat next to you in class? Save you a space at his lunch table? All good signs. If none of the above, then it's time to put out some of your own signals. Don't be afraid to speak up and start a conversation with him. He may like the same funny movie you saw yesterday or the same rock band. Be warm and friendly and keep things relaxed and casual. No pressure! Always remember one thing, though: Stay true to yourself and don't change who you are to impress this boy. He should like you for you.

XO,

Emma

Emma reread what she'd written and was pleased with it. Now she just had to post it and put her own plan into motion.

The next day, Emma decided she would wait outside the cafeteria and catch Jackson as he was walking into lunch. Maybe they could sit together, chat, and bond over the burger sliders. Maybe he'd finally open up to her and confess the reason behind his move from New York to Pennsylvania. She spotted him coming down the hall, his head buried in a math book.

"Hi!" she said, waving her hand in his face.

He looked up. "Hey, Emma."

"Whatcha got there?" she asked, pointing to his math book.

"Pre-algebra quiz next period. I have to study."

"Oh! I'm really good at math. I got a ninety-three on my last test—I can totally help you go over it."

Jackson looked puzzled. "Yeah, well, I'm just gonna go sit by myself and review." He paused. "By *myself*."

Emma ignored him and continued to press on. "There's sliders on the menu today—you definitely want to go for the cheeseburger and avoid the salad bar. The marinated veggies are soggy and gross."

"Thanks for the advice," he said and tried to push past her.

"You also want to steer clear of the sliced turkey—I found a hair on one of the slices the other day. Disgusting!"

"I'm not really all that hungry," Jackson replied. "I just need to sit down and study."

"Great! Where are you sitting?"

Jackson rolled his eyes. "Not with you, Emma. Sorry. I just can't be distracted."

Emma finally stopped talking. "Excuse me for trying to be helpful," she mumbled, walking away.

The entire lunch period she stared at Jackson and barely took a bite of her lunch. He was sitting by himself on a windowsill, flipping through his flash cards.

"Earth to Emma," Izzy said, elbowing her friend. "Can I have one of your fries?"

Emma didn't flinch or respond.

"Here, let me try," Harriet said. She cleared her throat. "So I read *Ask Emma* this morning. . . ."

Emma snapped out of her trance. "You did? Did you like it?"

"That was great advice you gave me, Em."

Emma shrugged. "Really? It doesn't seem to be working very well for me." She motioned toward Jackson, who seemed to be doing his very best to ignore her.

"Well, it worked for me!" Harriet exclaimed. "I did exactly what you said. I started a conversation with Marty about Comic Con. Turns out he's a huge Superman fan, and I love Wonder Woman. We're going together!"

Emma sighed. "Gee, that's great, Harriet. Glad I could help."

"You did! I'm posting a comment saying thanks. Then maybe no one will pay any attention to the other ones."

Emma's eyes widened. "*What* other ones?" She wanted to reach for her phone and read them herself, but she knew if Ms. Bates caught her, she'd be in big trouble.

"Nothing," Harriet said reassuringly. "Just some cranky people."

"Not again!" Emma moaned. "What did they write now?"

Harriet scratched her head, trying to recall. "Well, someone said they didn't need your advice in the love department. And someone else said your advice was pretty lame."

Emma banged her head on the cafeteria table. "Why is everyone determined to destroy my blog when all I want to do is make their lives better?"

"Do you want my opinion?" Izzy spoke up but didn't wait for Emma's reply. "I think people just don't like you butting in. No offense, Em."

Emma was getting more upset. "I'm not butting in. I'm advising. There's a difference."

Just then someone tapped her on the shoulder. He was a tall, athletic-looking boy, dressed in sweats and a track team shirt. "Hey," the student said. "You're *Ask Emma*, right?" He was in her grade, someone Emma had never spoken to but recognized.

"Yeah," Emma said hesitantly. "I'm . . . her."

"I've been looking for you," the boy continued.

Emma gulped. What was that supposed to mean? Was he one of the people posting negative comments about her? Was he about to insult her at lunch in front of everyone? She braced herself.

"So, I know you usually advise people on personal stuff, but I have a big problem with a school situation," he began.

Emma sat up in her seat, relieved that he wasn't there to make a scene. "Really? I can help you with any problem."

He took the seat next to her, shoving over Izzy. "I'm Xavier," he said.

"Gee, Xavier, am I in your way?" Izzy griped, trying not to fall off the bench.

"Kind of. I need to talk to Emma for a sec." He took a deep breath. "I think my Spanish teacher is totally unfair. Not only did he give us a pop quiz yesterday on stuff we never learned, but he's assigning a major term paper over Veterans Day weekend. I was supposed to go camping with my family, and now my plans are totally ruined."

Izzy smirked. "Bummer. You should have taken French."

"Izzy!" Emma silenced her BFF. "That is a big problem, Xavier. A wrong that needs righting!"

"So, you'll do something about it?" The boy's mood brightened. "I thought you might! Be at seventh-period Señor Gonzalez's class. See you there!"

Before Emma could say another word—or suggest he submit his issue to her in writing on the *Ask Emma* blog—he scooted away.

"So what are you going to tell Señor Gonzalez when you see him?" Izzy asked, chuckling.

"I have no idea!" Emma exclaimed. "I'm a blogger, not a referee. And my Spanish *no es bueno.*"

"But you always say that people can come to you with any problem—and he just did," Harriet pointed out.

"Fine. *Vamos* to seventh-period Spanish."

Izzy winced. "You might want to practice your verb conjugation first. *Vamos* means '*we* go.'"

"I know." Emma smiled. "You're both coming with me. If I have to try to reason with this teacher, I'm gonna need some backup."

Harriet looked at Izzy, who was shaking her head "no way."

"What if Señor Gonzalez isn't thrilled with our interfering?" Izzy asked. "What if he yells—or worse, sends us to Ms. Bates?"

"Best friends stick together," Emma pointed out. "Do I need to remind you about the time you tore a hole in the butt of your leggings and I gave you my hoodie to wrap around your waist?"

"That was different," Izzy huffed. "That was a fashion emergency—my butt was getting drafty."

Emma turned her attention to Harriet. "Or about the time you skinned your knee on the playground and I held your hand in the nurse's office because you said the sight of blood makes you faint?"

Harriet winced at the memory. "That was very nice of you—"

"That happened in first grade!" Izzy reminded her. "Like, six years ago!"

Emma waved her hand in the air. "It doesn't matter when it happened. The point is friends support each other through thick and thin."

Harriet nodded. "I'll do it. I'm in, Em."

Izzy sighed. "Fine, I can't argue with both of you. I'm in too—just promise not to get us all in trouble."

Emma smiled. "I'll do my best." Then she took

one last glance in Jackson's direction. He looked up from his notes for a split second, caught her eye, and smiled. Cracking the mystery of Jackson Knight was certainly a challenge—but that would have to wait till later. She had a bigger *problema* on her hands!

A few minutes into the start of seventh period, Emma, Izzy, and Harriet each asked to be excused from their classes to go to the nurse's office.

"I think I'm coming down with a cold." Emma coughed for emphasis at her English teacher, Mrs. Cole. "I feel kinda dizzy too—like the whole room is spinning."

She met her two friends outside Señor Gonzalez's Beginning Spanish class on the second floor.

"I'm pretty sure my chemistry teacher, Mrs. Lawrence, believed that I needed to go to the nurse," Izzy said.

"Did you cough and sneeze?" Harriet asked her.

Izzy shook her head. "No, I told her I felt itchy. Then I scratched my hair. She practically threw me out into the hallway."

Emma giggled. "Oh my gosh, she probably thought you have head lice!"

Izzy shrugged. "Whatever. It worked, didn't it?"

Emma peeked through the glass window in the classroom door—class was in session, and Señor Gonzalez looked intensely involved in teaching. She saw Xavier seated in the very back row of the classroom, anxiously watching the door for her arrival.

"Are you just going to stand there looking in?" Izzy asked her. "You told Xavier you were going to right wrongs."

Emma took a deep breath. "Don't rush me. I'm strategizing."

"What does that mean?" Harriet asked.

"It means she has no idea what she's going to do," Izzy said, sighing. "This is going to go badly, I can feel it."

"No, no, it won't," Emma assured them. "I just need a moment." She closed her eyes and tried to put herself in Señor Gonzalez's shoes. What did he want and need from his students? What was his motivation for the pop quizzes and extra homework on the long weekend? She looked at the faces of the students. A few yawned; one was fast asleep and drooling on his desk; several were doodling and passing notes.

"I see," she said suddenly.

"What? What do you see?" Harriet asked.

"I see the problem. I see where Señor is coming from." She knocked and then gently pushed the door open slightly.

"*Hola*," Señor Gonzalez said, noticing her head poking into his room. Thank goodness he didn't immediately chase her out!

Emma cleared her throat. She saw Xavier giving her a thumbs-up. "Um, excuse me for interrupting—I promise this won't take long. My name is Emma Woods. I write the *Ask Emma* advice blog?"

The teacher nodded. "*Sí, sí*. Mr. Goddard

mentioned that a student of his was writing a blog. How can we help you?"

"Actually, I'm here to help *you* with a problem." She motioned for Harriet and Izzy to fall in behind her. "Or as you would say in Spanish class, *un problema.*"

"*¡Ah, sí! ¡Bueno, habla español! Dime el problema.*"

Emma gulped. She was only in her second year of Spanish! Did he expect her to explain herself solely in *español*? That could be tricky, but if it meant he didn't kick her out . . .

"Um, I'll try," she stammered. "*La próxima semana es Veterans Day.*"

The teacher nodded. "*Sí, el Día de los Veteranos.*"

"Exactly!" Emma shouted, relieved he understood her. "*Su clase tiene* a major term *papel* to write. Which isn't fair, because it's a *tres-día* weekend, and some people have plans to go away." She realized she had been babbling in both English and Spanish.

Señor Gonzalez frowned. "*¿La clase quiere más tiempo?*"

"*¡Sí!* Exactly!" Emma said. "They need more time,

maybe just a day or *dos más*. That would be awesome!"

"That would be *increíble*," Izzy corrected her. "And don't forget about the pop quizzes while you're at it."

"Oh! Those too!" Emma said. "There are some concerns that you give too many pop quizzes. *Muchos exámenes . . . de* pop?"

Izzy groaned and Señor Gonzalez chuckled. He said, "*Claro*," put his book down, and sat on the edge of his desk. "You've been asked to bring *estas quejas*—these complaints—to my attention?"

"No—I mean, yes. But I'm not here to complain. I'm here to try to help everyone find a good solution. That's what I do. And I understand where you're coming from."

"Oh, you do?" he asked.

"Absolutely!" Emma responded. "I was watching from outside, and I could see that your class isn't doing a very good job of paying attention. And I'm sure you have to give pop quizzes to ensure they're doing the homework and they're up to speed with everything you're teaching in class."

He nodded. *"Sí, es correcto."*

"So I propose a compromise, something that will work for everyone," Emma continued. "Fewer pop quizzes and less homework on weekends if the class promises to pay attention, complete assignments on time . . . and no one can get below an eighty on any test."

A kid in the front row gasped. "An eighty? Are you kidding me? I almost failed my last test!"

"Then you'll have to study *mucho más*," Izzy scolded him. "Seriously!"

"I think that sounds reasonable," the teacher said. "But how do you propose we make sure everyone keeps up their part of the bargain?"

"Well, maybe everyone could sign a contract," Emma suggested.

"A contract?" Señor Gonzalez contemplated the suggestion. "That's an interesting concept."

"My dad is a lawyer, and he always says a contract ensures that both parties are equally represented," Harriet piped up.

"We could create a class contract," Emma continued. "I'll write it up and post it on my blog in case other students and teachers want to use it. It will include everyone's responsibilities. And as a show of good faith, maybe you could postpone the paper so everyone could enjoy *el Día de los Veteranos* weekend?"

Señor Gonzalez considered for a moment. "I am willing to do that if everyone in class signs the contract—and starts participating more. That way I won't have to give so many pop quizzes."

"Yes!" Xavier pumped his fist in the air. "I can go camping."

"Now, do you suppose we can get back to our lesson," the teacher asked his class, "unless there are any other issues *Ask Emma* can help us solve?"

Emma smiled. It felt good to be acknowledged. It felt good to make a difference in the lives of her fellow students. This was what she had wanted to do all along, and now, for the first time, people were willing to give her a chance.

A girl's hand went up. "Does this contract thing

work for parents too?" she asked Emma. "Mine have a ridiculous curfew for me on the weekends. Who has to be home at eight o'clock when you're thirteen?"

"Well, my parents won't let me have a cell phone!" said another student. "What do I do about that?"

"You think you've got problems?" said another boy, sighing. "My basketball coach always benches me. How do I get him to put me back in the game?"

"My best friend is mad at me because she thinks I'm talking about her behind her back," another girl volunteered. "How do I get my bestie back?"

"All excellent questions . . . Put 'em in an email," Izzy said, guiding Emma out the door before the teacher lost his patience. "Feel free to *Ask Emma*! *¡Adiós!*"

"Well, that was *muy loco*," Izzy said when they were safely out of the Spanish room and seated on a bench in the schoolyard. "If we didn't get you out of there, you would have been solving problems for the rest of the class—maybe the rest of the week!"

"It was amazing," Emma said. She couldn't wipe the grin off her face. "So many kids, so many problems!"

"It made my head hurt," Harriet said. "Everyone and their issues—ouch!"

"I love it. It's like solving a math equation," Emma said. "At least that's how I see it. What can you add or subtract to make things work out so they're balanced on both sides?"

"I don't like math," Harriet said, rubbing her temples.

"Do you think there's more where that came from?" Emma asked her friends.

"Problems? In middle school? Are you kidding?" Izzy said. "There isn't one kid here who doesn't have *some* problems."

Emma felt like she'd made tremendous progress

today—her fellow students were starting to trust her and ask her advice. Sure, there were a few who didn't care or like what she had to say. But there were just as many, maybe more, who did.

"Okay," she said, standing up. "Enough wasting time. I have to go write that class contract on my blog like I promised."

"Aw, you're no fun," Izzy protested. "We got out of seventh period and I have ten minutes before I have to leave for gymnastics. Can't we just sit and chill?"

A shadow suddenly loomed over them. "What do you mean you got out of seventh period?" It was Ms. Bates, the principal. "Are you three cutting class?"

Emma looked over at her two friends. Harriet's face was so pale that Emma was afraid she might pass out. As for Izzy, all she could do was chew her gum loudly and stare at Ms. Bates in horror.

"I'm waiting for an answer, ladies," the principal said, tapping her foot. "Why are you milling around the yard?"

"I'm sorry," Emma began. "It's my fault—I made them come with me. I can explain."

"Fine," Ms. Bates said. "I look forward to hearing your explanation today after school . . . in detention."

"You promised you wouldn't get us in trouble!" Izzy moaned as they walked into the detention room. There were already several students there, looking equally miserable. "My mom is going to kill me! I've never gotten detention before. This is humiliating! And I'm going to miss gymnastics practice."

Emma didn't know what to do or say about the

situation. Clearly, Ms. Bates was furious that she'd found them out of class—and intended to make a point. But wasn't this taking things a bit too far?

"I can't be in detention either," Harriet cried. "I have my piano lesson at four, and I'm gonna miss the last school bus home." She was in tears, wringing her hands.

"Guys, let's not panic," Emma said, trying to calm her friends down. "I'll talk to Ms. Bates and explain."

"Maybe you shouldn't explain, Emma," Harriet said. "Maybe you shouldn't talk at all. Because when you do, things have a habit of going wrong."

"Wait, are you *Ask Emma*?" interrupted one of the students in the room. He jumped out of his seat and came over. "You write an advice blog, right? You solve everyone's problems?"

"Maybe," Emma said cautiously. He was a year younger, a sixth grader who had a reputation for getting sent to the principal's office for misbehaving.

"I shouldn't be here—can you help me?" he asked.

Emma looked into his dark brown eyes—they seemed sincere.

"Tell me about it!" Izzy grumped. "I don't belong

here either—I just listened to Emma and look where it got me." She took a seat at a desk in the back of the room next to Harriet, who was nervously chewing on her fingernails.

"Don't do it, Em," Harriett begged her. "No more helping. We're in enough trouble already."

Emma ignored her friends' pleas. Here was someone who needed her help, and she wasn't about to turn her back on him. "What can I do for you?" she asked the boy.

"Ugh!" Izzy exclaimed. "Here we go again!" She rested her elbows on the desk and covered her ears.

"I didn't do anything wrong," the boy insisted. "I shouldn't be here. It's not my fault."

"What's not your fault?" Emma asked.

He leaned in closer to tell her his tale. "I was in the cafeteria, and I was hurrying so I wouldn't be late to my next period. I guess I forgot, and I left the tray with all my garbage and silverware on it, and the lunch lady caught me . . . and here I am."

"You left your lunch tray," Emma said. "That's it? That's all you did?"

"I know," the boy said. "Crazy, right?"

"I'm in here for chewing gum in PE," another girl said. "I was about to swallow it and Coach Hawkins didn't even give me a chance!"

"I've got all of you beat," said another student. "I'm in here for burping."

Emma had to cover her mouth to keep from laughing—that was the most ridiculous reason for getting detention she'd ever heard!

"It was right in the middle of our English vocab quiz, and I couldn't help it—I always burp when I'm nervous. Ms. Churchill thought I did it on purpose to disrupt the class."

When Ms. Bates came into the room, everyone got quiet and squirmed in their seats. All Emma could hear was Harriet sniffling.

"Ms. Bates?" Emma asked, raising her hand. "May I tell you something, please?"

The principal motioned for her to approach the front of the classroom. "Is this the explanation you were going to share with me for why you cut Mrs.

Cole's English class?" Emma gulped. Ms. Bates made it sound a lot worse than it was.

"We didn't actually *cut* . . . we excused ourselves to go to the nurse," she said.

"And did you go to the nurse? Are you ill?" Ms. Bates asked.

"No, we kind of got sidetracked," Emma said. "We had to go to Señor Gonzalez's Spanish class and help a student."

"Help a student? How?" Ms. Bates tapped her fingernails on the desk.

"Well, you see, I write this advice blog for the seventh grade, and one of the kids asked if I could fix a problem in his class. So I had this idea of creating a class contract so the students would know what was expected of them and Señor Gonzalez would give them less homework on the weekend and fewer pop quizzes."

Ms. Bates pursed her lips. "A class contract?"

"Like a lawyer," Emma said. "It was just an idea."

"It's an interesting one," the principal said.

"You know, a contract might be helpful for detention too," Emma suggested.

Ms. Bates crossed her arms over her chest. "And what are you suggesting, Ms. Woods?"

"Well, maybe if there was a written contract of rules, like no chewing gum in PE or faking a trip to the nurse or ditching your lunch tray—"

"You forgot the burping," the boy piped up from the back of the room. "That's an important one."

Ms. Bates considered. "You're proposing that students would agree that if they violated these rules, they would have to go to detention?"

"Right. They'd sign a contract acknowledging they know what the rules are and what happens if they break them. But I think a lot of kids wouldn't break them if they had a list of what not to do."

"I'll think it over," Ms. Bates said.

"Does this mean we don't have to stay here?" Harriet asked hopefully.

"I suppose your heart was in the right place,

trying to help your peers," Ms. Bates added. "But I don't ever want to find any of you cutting class again. Is that clear? You only get off the hook once."

Izzy was already on her feet and halfway out the door. "Crystal clear! Thank you!" she said, pulling Harriet along with her.

"Thank you, Ms. Bates," Emma said. "I really didn't mean for this to happen this way."

"I know you're eager to help others, Emma," the principal replied. "But always consider the means to that end."

Emma nodded, and Ms. Bates released the rest of the students as well with a stern warning.

"Wow, you are amazing, *Ask Emma*," said Burping Boy as he scrambled out of the room. "I'm definitely writing to you if I have another problem in school."

Emma went to her locker to get her jacket so she could catch the school bus. She dug her phone out of a pocket and signed on to her blog to check if there were any new comments. She was hoping for some more of the glowing thank-yous she'd received today—at least one or two praising her for her efforts in Señor Gonzalez's class and detention. But instead someone had written a note filled with bold, capitalized words. She read them slowly, one by one, letting them sink in:

KEEP YOUR DUMB IDEAS TO YOURSELF. WHO DO YOU THINK YOU ARE? JUST SOME STUPID KNOW-IT-ALL WHO KNOWS NOTHING!

Her heart pounded and her hands shook, but she managed to delete every word. How could someone write this about her? Mr. Goddard had told her to ignore and delete any negative comments, and she had. Still, she couldn't erase the words from her mind: *SOME STUPID KNOW-IT-ALL WHO KNOWS NOTHING!* It made her feel sad, small, insignificant. Even though they were just words, they stung. She could hear her mom's voice in her head reminding her, "Sticks and stones . . ." She'd taught her that way back in kindergarten, when a boy at the playground made fun of her freckles and called her "polka-dot face." But these words—maybe because they were written on a webpage for all to see—hurt. They did more than hurt; Emma felt like someone had just slapped her across the face and left five fingerprints across her cheek.

She walked to the school bus stop, trying to shake off the feeling. She saw Elton at the back of the line, waiting as well. He had earphones on and was grooving to a tune only he could hear. Maybe that's what she needed to do—tune out the negativity and the world in general.

"Hey," he said, noticing her behind him. "What's up?"

She smiled back weakly. "Nothing."

He took off his earphones so they could talk. "Did Jackson tell you about the cool science project we're cooking up?"

So they *had* partnered up in lab after her failed attempt to get Harriet and Elton together. "No, he didn't mention it." There were probably a lot of things Jackson hadn't shared with her. At this point, she was just happy he was speaking to her at all.

"Well, it's awesome. It's totally going to win the science fair this year," Elton bragged.

To be polite, Emma pretended to be interested in his latest scientific endeavor, even if it was the furthest thing from her mind at the moment: "Uh-huh. Sounds good."

"Get this: the Chemistry of Ice Cream," Elton continued. "It's about molecular weight and adding chemicals to ice to make it freeze faster."

Emma nodded. "Cool."

"Ha! Cool! That's funny—'cause ice cream is cool," Elton said, chuckling to himself.

Emma wasn't trying to be funny. She was too busy surveying the line of middle schoolers waiting for the bus, wondering which one of them might have written the comment on her blog. It could have been anyone: that girl with the glasses chatting with her friends, the boy with the baseball hat on backward. Even Elton! That was the terrible thing about social media—it allowed people to hide behind the mask of their phone or tablet or computer screen. They could do or say anything without having to reveal themselves. She had asked Mr. Goddard to allow students to submit anonymously so they wouldn't be embarrassed to share their problems. But that went for their comments as well. She would never know who was secretly hating her.

"Did you happen to read my blog recently?" she asked Elton, hoping to rule him out.

"Your blog? Um, no, sorry. I've been too busy with soccer practice and our science fair project."

That seemed reasonable. So maybe Elton wasn't the culprit. But that left more than two hundred other kids as possibilities.

"What did you write?" he asked her.

"It's not what I wrote, it's what someone wrote about it," she tried to explain. "It was awful."

"So just delete it."

It sounded so easy and simple when he put it that way. "But I read it," she insisted. "It's too late. It's burned in my brain."

"Forget about it. I mean, anyone who writes a mean comment online is just too scared to say it to your face."

"Scared?" Emma asked. "Of me?"

"Probably," Elton said, shrugging. "Why else would they post something anonymously?"

He did have a good point—and if they were scared of her, she certainly didn't need to be scared of them.

"Besides," Elton tried to assure her, "it's just one comment, one person's take on it. My photography teacher once wrote on my report card, 'Perhaps Elton needs to wear his glasses more often—his focus seems to be off.' I know he meant it as constructive criticism, but I was really offended at first. I like my photos fuzzy. But in the end, he gave me an A and told me my work was avant-garde."

Emma remembered seeing some of Elton's

pictures on display at the student art show last semester and wondered why his self-portrait was a blur. He had done it on purpose!

"You're right," she said, considering his words. "It is just one person, not the entire middle school. And people can change their minds."

Elton tuned to another song. "Exactly. If someone doesn't like your music, they don't have to listen." He handed her his earphones.

She put them on and heard a string quartet blaring through them. "Really? You like classical?" she asked, surprised. She didn't know any kids their age who liked classical music.

"Beethoven is my jam," he said. "Although Mozart is my go-to dude for singing in the shower."

The bus pulled into the stop, and Emma realized she was feeling better. Talking to Elton had put things into perspective—one person's voice was no stronger or more important than hers. Sticks and stones . . .

#

When she got home, she went straight to her computer, promising herself she would only type the class contract into her blog—not skim down below her posts to see if anyone had anymore to say. But then she caught herself paging down and spying a new comment someone had left. It read:

> Emma, you're a lifesaver! I talked to my parents today after school about us all signing a curfew contract. I promised I would tell them where I was going and who I was with, and text every couple of hours so they wouldn't worry. They agreed to let me stay out next Saturday till 10:00! I can go to the movies with my friends! I owe it all to you!

Emma read it once again, then a third and fourth time—it was her very first fan letter! She had done it! She had helped someone! She felt like jumping up and down on her bed but figured her mom would probably come in and scold her. Instead, she typed a reply:

Good for you! So glad I could help, and keep those questions and problems coming!

XO,

Emma

UP IN THE AIR

Nobody at Austen Middle liked PE class—not even Emma, who was on the tennis team and didn't think exercise was evil or messed up hair and makeup. Maybe it was because they spent almost thirty minutes of the forty-five-minute period doing boring warm-ups and not actually playing a sport.

"I can't move," Harriet moaned after twenty

jumping jacks. "This is torture!" She collapsed in a heap on the gymnasium floor.

Coach Hawkins blew her whistle. "On your feet, Harriet," she barked. "Push-ups next. Drop and give me twenty."

"This is so unfair," Jordana Fairfax chimed in. She was petite and pretty with honey-colored hair and green eyes. She and Emma had been friends back in first grade—they played with Barbies all the time after school. But over the years, they'd grown apart, probably because Jordie was so focused on appearances (her own in particular) and her popularity. Now she kind of *looked* like a Barbie doll and had a group of girls who followed her around, hanging on her every word.

"My manicure is getting ruined!" Jordie told Coach Hawkins, waving a chipped thumbnail at her. "And I just had a mani/pedi yesterday!" The coach ignored her.

"Ooh, love that color," Harriet gushed. "What is it?"

"Tutu Cute," Jordie replied, examining the rest of her pale pink nails for flaws. "I cannot do push-ups on these hardwood floors. It's a health hazard." She turned to Emma. "Aren't you supposed to be a problem solver? Can't you do something about this?"

Emma beamed. Was her reputation for problem-solving getting around the school? Was Jordie, one of the popular girls, welcoming her assistance?

Jordie snapped her fingers in Emma's face. "Are you gonna just stand there or go tell the coach to stop making me sweat?" She gave Emma a little shove toward Coach Hawkins, who was now insisting a group of girls climb a rope hanging from the ceiling. Each one skidded down after going up a few inches.

"Excuse me, Coach Hawkins?" Emma approached her gently. "Can I talk to you a sec?"

"No, you can't go to the bathroom or the nurse," Coach snapped back. "No excuses to get out of my class."

"Oh, I wasn't trying to. I don't mind PE like everyone else. I'm on the tennis team."

Coach Hawkins looked her over. "Okay then. What is it today?"

"Well, I was wondering. . . . Do you think we could start playing volleyball soon? I think everyone is getting tired from the warm-up."

Coach Hawkins put her hands on her hips. "Are you trying to get out of push-ups too?"

"No! I'm just excited to play!" Emma smiled, hoping *anything* she was saying was convincing.

"All right," Coach Hawkins said, blowing her whistle. "Enough with the warm-ups. Everybody in the center for volleyball."

Emma turned proudly to Jordie. "You're welcome," she said.

"For what? You want me to thank you for making us play volleyball? When I could get hit in the face with the ball and get a black eye?"

"That's way worse than a chipped nail," Lyla, one of Jordie's minions, said, nodding.

Jordie turned to her friends. "This is what she calls helping. Such a joke. She made it worse!"

Emma was determined. "You asked me to get her to stop the push-ups, and I did. You didn't say anything about volleyball."

"I want PE to be over early." Jordie sighed. "But if you can't do that . . . I guess your *Ask Emma* blog isn't worth reading."

Emma felt Harriet's hand on her shoulder. "Don't, Em," she whispered. "Whatever you're thinking, don't do it."

Emma saw the clock on the wall, hanging just underneath the ropes on the opposite side of the gym. All she had to do was get up there and give the minute hand a little push and . . .

She waited till everyone had formed their teams on either side of the net to talk to Coach Hawkins again.

"Coach," she said, tapping her on the back.

"What is it now, Emma?"

"I didn't get a chance to climb the rope, and I really wanted to practice. I'm just warming the bench right now waiting to be rotated in, so would you mind?"

"Well, okay. You need someone to spot you," Coach warned her.

Emma grabbed Harriet by the hand and pulled her over. "I've got a spotter!"

"Ow!" a voice shouted from the volleyball game.

Everyone turned to see Hailey covering her face. "Victoria spiked the ball at me!"

"One climb, then back to the game," Coach told Emma, before she hurried over to tend to Hailey.

Jordie shot Emma a dirty look. "You better fix this," she told her.

Emma dragged Harriet over to the ropes. The clock was about six feet off the ground, and if Emma climbed up, she might be able to reach it.

"You're gonna climb all the way up there?" Harriet gasped. "Are you crazy, Em? It's not worth it to impress Jordie!"

"I'm not trying to impress her," Emma insisted. "I'm trying to prove that I'm a woman of my word. If I say I'll fix a problem, I will."

"You're not a woman. You just turned thirteen,"

Harriet reminded her as Emma took hold of the rope with two hands.

"I can do it," Emma said, wrapping her feet around the bottom as she had seen the other girls try to do. She tugged and pulled, but managed to get only an inch above the ground.

"Am I close?" she asked Harriet.

"Oh, I'd say you've got about five feet, eleven inches more to go."

Emma planted her sneakers back on the gymnasium floor. "You're gonna have to give me a boost," she told Harriet. "Get down and let me climb on your shoulders."

"My shoulders?" Harriet squeaked. "You never said anything about giving you a piggyback ride!"

"I just need a lift and I can make it the rest of the way," she assured her friend, climbing onto her back but accidentally stepping on her hair.

"Ouch!" Harriet yelped. "Em, watch it!"

"Almost there," Emma said, pulling herself up the rope with all her might. She was now mere inches from the clock, hanging on for dear life. There was no way she could reach the clock hands. Not from this distance.

"Swing the rope over to the right," she instructed her friend. "Give it a good push so I get really close."

Harriet obeyed, and Emma flew into the wall, slamming it hard with her shoulder.

"Yow! Not that hard!" she called to her. "A nice, light swing so I can reach the clock."

Harriet tried again. And again. And again. Emma was now swinging like a pendulum, unable to grab hold of the clock for fear of letting go.

"You have to reach out with one arm while you hold on with the other," Harriet called up to her. "Hurry, before Coach Hawkins notices!"

Emma wasn't sure she could maintain her grip with just one hand, but there didn't seem to be any other choice. "Okay," she said. "Here goes nothing." She released her right hand and suddenly felt her left hand slipping down the rope.

Uh-oh, she thought to herself, *this isn't good*. But

before she could warn Harriet to look out below, she lost her grip on the rope and landed with a crash on top of her bestie. Coach Hawkins raced over to see if they were injured.

"What happened? Are you both okay?" Coach asked.

Harriet was lying on her back, staring up at the ceiling. "I think so," she said. "Em, are you okay?"

Emma got up and suddenly swooned, dropping to the floor next to her. "Is the room spinning?" she asked. "Are those twinkly stars on the ceiling? Or are they butterflies?"

Coach Hawkins looked concerned. "Okay, class is over. You two girls, don't move. I'm going to get the nurse."

She ran out the door of the gym as Emma suddenly sat up. She looked at Jordie, who was standing over her, speechless. "Now you're welcome," Emma said.

"You mean you faked the fall?" Jordie asked her.

"No, the fall was real," Emma replied. "I faked being hurt. When the nurse comes, I'll tell her I'm fine."

"That was amazing! You're amazing!" Jordie cheered. "You actually know what you're doing, Emma." She skipped off with her friends to the locker room to change—ten minutes before class was supposed to end. Harriet sat up; she didn't look as happy as Jordie.

"Really? Faking an injury? Scamming Coach Hawkins? Emma, you're out of control," her friend said. "There has to be a better way to keep your promises."

Emma helped Harriet to her feet. "I know, I know, but I had to think fast." She noticed Harriet's hair was all rumpled and her glasses were twisted and hanging off her nose. She straightened them and pushed them back in place. "I'm sorry you had to break my fall, Harriet. What would I ever do without you?"

"I guess it was kind of partially my fault for telling you to let go," Harriet admitted. "But next time you want me to be your landing pad, give me a little warning first."

Coach Hawkins and Ms. Perry, the nurse, came running. "Are you okay, dear?" Nurse Perry asked Emma.

"I'm fine," Emma assured them both. "I just lost my grip."

After Ms. Perry checked her and Harriet head to toe, Emma promised to take it easy and steer clear of rope climbing during PE.

She glanced at the clock. It was two fifteen and she was already late to English class.

"Great," Harriet said with a sigh. "We got Jordie out early, and now we're both late to seventh period! I'm starting to hate your blog, Ems!"

Emma raced up the stairs to class with Harriet trailing behind her. She was starting to like her blog a lot more.

Word got around fast at Austen Middle—particularly when Jordie was spreading it. Lucky for Emma, she was singing her praises—especially to students who wanted to get out of a biology test, an assembly period, or an oral presentation on the ancient world.

"So my report is next Monday," Marcus, another seventh grader, told her. He waited at her locker—

Jordie had pointed out which one it was—ready to pounce on her with his problem. "Can you maybe make the period end a little early like you did for Jordie—so I only have to talk for a few minutes? I'm not really good with public speaking."

Emma frowned—she didn't want kids thinking of her as a get-out-of-class-free pass. "I have a better idea," she suggested. "Why don't you take some deep breaths, focus on one person, not the whole class in front of you, and speak directly to him or her? That should help your jitters."

Marcus stared. "You're saying you won't help me then?"

"I just gave you a bunch of great tips," she insisted. "I *am* trying to help you."

He stormed off, unhappy with her response. And there was more where that came from. Emma found herself having to turn down several more cries for help that might get her sent to detention again.

"But you don't understand," Lyla pleaded with her one morning before homeroom. "My favorite pop star, Shawn Mendes, is going to be on the *Early Morning Show*, and I need to go to the TV studio super-early and try and meet him in person. Can't you talk to my social studies teacher and get her to mark me on time if I'm just forty minutes late?"

Emma shook her head. "That would leave five minutes of class. Why bother?"

"Oh, okay!" Lyla said cheerfully. "I'll just skip it altogether and you'll take care of it?"

Emma pouted. "No, Lyla. That's not going to work either."

Lyla walked off in a huff.

"You did the right thing. You have to be very selective," Izzy told her friend. "You can't help everyone. It has to be someone who really needs it— and not just because they're too lazy to do homework or don't want to go to class." Izzy shuffled off to class, leaving her bestie with a lot to think about. Emma knew Izzy was right; she had to be careful of her peers' motivations. But she didn't know how she would weed out the people who really, truly, desperately needed her from the rest of the pack.

She headed to class when a girl suddenly jumped in front of her. "You're *Ask Emma*, aren't you?"

"Yes," Emma answered. The girl was one of Jordie's followers. She'd seen her with their clique in the cafeteria, hanging on the queen bee's every word.

"I'm Saige," the girl introduced herself. "And I have a major problem."

"If Jordie sent you . . ." Emma hesitated.

"No! I don't want Jordie to know anything about this. I'd be mortified."

Now Emma was curious—this sounded serious. "Okay, how can I help?" she asked.

"I'm trying out for the cheerleading squad. Jordie and Lyla are co-captains and they're adding new girls to the team. I take acro at my dance studio every Saturday, so I know I'd be great. I can even do a front aerial and a toe touch."

"I'm not following," Emma said. "If you can do all that, then you'll get picked for the cheer squad for sure. What's the problem?"

"Promise you won't tell," Saige whispered.

Emma nodded, and Saige led her into the girls' bathroom. She checked to make sure it was empty, then swept her long, dark hair back off her face.

"Still not following," Emma said.

"My ears," she whispered.

"What do your ears have to do with anything?"

Saige leaned over to check that no one was in a toilet stall. "They stick out—can't you see?" she insisted. "When I wear a ponytail, I look like Dumbo!"

"So don't wear a ponytail," Emma suggested. "I mean, there are a lot of other hairstyles out there. I just read in *Seventeen* that a long bob is all the rage."

"Not for cheer. You have to wear a ponytail—it's a rule. I'm so embarrassed, I'm sure I'll mess up if everyone starts staring at my ears!"

Emma shook her head. "They're really not bad. Honestly, if you hadn't pointed them out, I never would have noticed."

"Well, I notice. And I know Jordie will notice. You have to help me!"

Emma thought a moment. Could they tape Saige's ears back? Glue them? Just long enough to get Saige through the tryouts? Maybe a big sombrero? "How have you camouflaged them up until now?" she asked.

"With long layers around my face—and the occasional cute beanie," Saige said. "But I can't wear my hair down or wear a hat when I'm doing cartwheels in front of Jordie and Lyla. I'll look like a freak! I need another idea." She bent down to tie her sneaker shoelace—and something suddenly dawned on Emma.

"Okay, meet me after school and I'll ask my mom to drive us to the mall," she told Saige. "I think I know how we can hide your ears in a very fashionable way."

"If you can pull this off by tomorrow's tryouts, I'll owe you big time," Saige said. "But no one can know about this."

Emma zipped her lips. "I promise not to breathe a word."

Emma led Saige to the second floor of the mall, where she knew there was one store that might hold the solution to her problem. The sign on the window read "Accessories R Us." Saige peered inside—there were rows and rows of earrings, necklaces, hats, and bags. Emma held up a pair of large gold hoops. "How cool are these?" she asked. "Izzy's birthday is next month. I wonder if she'd like them."

Saige grabbed her by the shoulders. "Focus," she said. "The last thing I am buying is a pair of earrings that will draw attention to my ears."

Emma led her to the aisle she was thinking of, where dozens of hooks displayed a collection of chiffon and silk scarves in every possible color and pattern. She chose a pink one and tied it with a big floppy bow over Saige's head, covering her ears. "I got the idea when you tied your shoelace. You could pull your hair back in a ponytail and tie a scarf on like this. That way no one will see your ears." She turned Saige to face the mirror.

"That's a really big bow," Saige said hesitantly.

"But it's pink," Emma reminded her. "You can't

go wrong with pink." At least she was pretty sure that was what Jordie would think.

"I guess," Saige said. "It's kinda early-eighties Madonna."

"Problem solved!" Emma assured her. "Coordinate your outfit to match and your tryout will be a success."

Saige handed the salesperson the scarf. "I'll take it—but this better work."

The next day, as soon as the last-period bell rang, Emma raced to the gymnasium so she could watch the cheer team tryouts. She was running through the third-floor double doors when she collided with Jackson, who was heading in the opposite direction.

"Whoa!" he said. "Where's the fire?"

"No fire, cheer tryouts," Emma replied. "I've only got a few minutes before they start."

Jackson raised an eyebrow. "You? You're trying out to be a cheerleader?"

Emma started to brush off the comment and continue on her way when she suddenly considered what he was saying. "Wait, what's wrong with me being a cheerleader?"

"Everything. You're just not the type."

Now Emma was annoyed. "And what type is that exactly—that I'm not?" Was he insinuating she wasn't pretty enough? Coordinated enough? Cheerful enough?

"You know. Most of those cheer girls are only concerned with how they look."

This was getting worse by the minute! "You don't think I care what I look like?" Emma exclaimed. "Well, that's awfully nice of you."

"No, I don't mean it like that. I just mean you're not the kind of person who only thinks about fashion and makeup and her hair."

Emma looked down at her outfit—she was wearing a pair of ripped jeans and a simple black tee. Her nails were unpolished, and her hair was up in a messy bun. She could see why Jackson might think she didn't have cheerleader potential—she was a wreck! But did he really have to point it out? "Thanks for the vote of confidence," she grumped.

"Emma, it's not an insult!" Jackson insisted.

"Really? Because it sure sounds like it."

"I'm just saying you're more serious than those cheerleader girls."

Serious? Was he saying she was too boring or intense? The more Jackson said, the worse she felt!

"I have to go now," she said, pushing past him. "Even if you think cheerleading is out of my league."

"No! You don't get it! You're out of *their* league!" he called after her.

Emma froze in her tracks. Okay, that sounded almost like he was being nice. "You really think that?" she asked, turning around to face him.

"Well, yeah," Jackson said. "You're not like those other girls. And it's a good thing."

Emma noticed his cheeks were flushed—was he blushing? "I'm not trying out," she told him. "I'm going to *watch* tryouts. I helped one of the girls with a problem, and I want to make sure it goes smoothly."

"Oh," he said. "So there you go. I was right. I knew it."

Emma rolled her eyes—it was just like him to turn this into a told-ya-so moment. Jackson Knight was totally infuriating! She watched him walk away, and then it occurred to her: he was also totally adorable.

But that thought would have to wait till later—tryouts were already starting.

Emma burst into the gym and saw a group of girls lined up in formation in front of a panel consisting of Jordie, Lyla, and Coach Hawkins. Emma took a seat in the back of the bleachers and spotted Saige in the second row of girls. It was easy—she was the only one with a giant pink bow on her head.

Jordie had a clipboard and was checking off names. When she called "Saige Dixon," Saige stepped forward and smiled brightly.

"Why are you wearing that thing?" Jordie asked, pointing to her hair.

"Um, I thought it was a bold fashion statement," Saige replied. "And it matches my outfit."

Jordie pursed her lips and thought for a moment.

"I suppose," she said. Then she moved on to the next girl.

Hooray! Emma thought. This was actually going to work! Saige looked calmer too. At least Jordie hadn't made her take off the scarf or laughed in her face.

When it was time for the actual tryout, Lyla hit a button on a portable speaker, and music filled the gym. Jordie ran through a complicated routine of steps and kicks. "We want to see how you would add to it," she told the girls. "So freestyle the ending with some moves that show us what you've got."

This was great, Emma thought. Saige would wow them with one of her acro tricks and they'd surely offer her a spot. Emma watched as the candidates struggled to remember what Jordie had demonstrated. Only Saige seemed confident—she stood out from everyone, and Jordie's eyes were fixed on her, Emma noticed.

Then it was time for the freestyle section. Saige did an amazing backflip and broke into a jaw-dropping series of tumbles. Everything was going well, but then Emma saw the scarf slip off the top of Saige's head mid-flip. It was hanging in front of her eyes like a blindfold, but there was nothing she could do to fix it. Not now, not in the middle of her routine. The rest of the events seemed to unfold in slow motion. Saige's cartwheel was off center, and she knocked over the two girls next to her. Then she tripped the two girls in front of her and did a front aerial practically into the judges' laps! Coach Hawkins looked horrified; Jordie and Lyla were out of their seats, ducking behind her. The music came to an end, and Saige managed to pull the scarf off her eyes and place it back on her head. She looked around. Girls were lying on the ground, and steam was coming out of Jordie's ears.

"Are you crazy, Saige?" Jordie said. "You almost killed us!"

"It was an accident," Saige tried to apologize. "I just couldn't see very well and got turned around . . . I'm really good at acro, honest," she pleaded with them.

Emma felt terrible. The scarf had caused this

whole problem—and it had been all her idea. She stood up in the bleachers and shouted, "It's my fault! Not hers. Saige would make an amazing cheerleader. I told her to wear the scarf to cover her ears!" As soon as the words left her lips, she regretted them.

"Her ears? Why would you cover your ears?" Jordie asked Saige.

Oh no! Emma thought. This was what Saige had been afraid of all along! Emma ran over to stand by her side.

"You promised!" Saige shouted at Emma. "You said you wouldn't tell!"

"I didn't mean to!" Emma cried. "I was just trying to get them to give you another chance."

Jordie couldn't take the suspense any longer. "Okay, what is up with your ears?" she asked. "Take off the bow."

"I . . . I can't!" Saige's eyes filled with tears and she ran out of the gym. Coach Hawkins ran after her.

Emma didn't know what to say—this was a disaster. "She's really self-conscious about wearing a ponytail," she stammered. "You have to believe me! They don't look like Dumbo's at all!"

Jordie's eyes grew wide. "Dumbo? They look like elephant ears?"

"No! They don't. But she *thinks* they do. Please, you have to give her a spot on the team!"

Jordie took her seat next to Lyla and whispered something to her. They both laughed. Emma had a sinking feeling she'd made things worse, not better for Saige. This was a complete disaster!

Back home at night, she sat down at her laptop to write a blog post. It was what she should have told Saige all along. Now it was too late; the damage was done. But maybe it would get through to someone else. Maybe there was a lesson they could all learn from this.

No one is perfect. We all have our flaws and insecurities. Take me for example: I used to hate my freckles. I tried everything for years to hide them. I borrowed my mom's concealer and foundation and slathered it on. I even put lemon juice all over my nose and cheeks to try to get rid of them. (FYI, it doesn't work; you just end up smelling like a tropical fruit cup.) I wish I had remembered this when someone recently asked me to help them cover up something they didn't like about their appearance. I thought I was doing the right thing. But it backfired. And here's why: you should never be embarrassed of what makes you . . . you. Without these things, we'd all be boring clones. You should love who you are and embrace what makes you unique and special. And remember, we all hate stuff about ourselves sometimes. That's what makes us human. Don't be afraid to let people see the real you.

CHAPTER 10

LIAR, LIAR

The last thing Emma expected to see was Saige standing on the front steps to the school in a blue-and-white Austen Owls cheerleading jacket. But there she was one morning a few days later, laughing with Jordie and Lyla as if nothing had happened at tryouts.

"Saige! You made the team!" Emma exclaimed, running up to her.

Saige sniffed. "No thanks to you. You tried to sabotage me."

Emma was stunned. "Sabotage you? I was trying to help!"

"Yeah, like you helped me get out of social studies," Lyla reminded her. "Thanks for nothing. I missed meeting Shawn Mendes face-to-face."

Jordie gasped. "No, you didn't!"

"I did!" Lyla insisted. "And it was all her fault. She ruins everything." She pointed a finger accusingly at Emma.

"I didn't ruin anything," Emma insisted.

"Really? Whose idea was it to put that huge bow on Saige's head?" Jordie asked her.

Emma gulped. "Well, mine, but—"

"See! I told you!" Saige said. "She said my ears stuck out like Dumbo's and I'd never make the cheer squad unless I listened to her."

"Horrible," Lyla said. "You made her feel bad about herself when she's one of the best cheerleaders we've ever had on this team."

"And she's gonna win us the national cheerleading competition this year with those acro tricks," Jordie said, putting an arm around Saige. "I'm so glad Coach Hawkins persuaded you to come back and try out again for us—without the bow. How could we have known you were bullied into wearing it?"

"'Bullied'?" Emma was losing her temper—none of this was true! "I did nothing to bully her!"

"Well, you told us she looked like Dumbo," Jordie pointed out. "I heard it—didn't you, Lyla?"

"Totally! There's nothing wrong with her ears— why would you say such a horrible thing?"

Emma noticed that Saige was self-consciously twirling a strand of hair around her finger. She had let a few loose tendrils hang over her ears—her way of subtly camouflaging them. Emma knew the truth; she knew Saige was the one who'd been insecure and begged her to do something.

Why did I offer to help Saige in the first place? Emma fumed. *Why did I stick out my neck for someone who didn't appreciate it—and now she's turning on me?*

"Saige, please tell them the truth," Emma pleaded with her.

Saige took a deep breath. "The truth is I was really excited to try out for the team, and I told Emma. That's when she decided to destroy my chances."

"Liar!" Emma shouted at her. "You know that's not what happened!"

Harriet and Izzy came over to see what the commotion was about.

"You okay, Em?" Izzy asked her.

"You're the one who's a liar," Jordie tossed back at Emma. "You wrote on your blog that you should always let people see the real you. Then you made Saige feel embarrassed about how she looks."

Harriet looked at Emma, surprised. "Did you really do that, Em?"

"Of course not!" Emma protested.

"You did take her to the mall to get that ridiculous scarf, didn't you?" Jordie asked. "You never once told her, and I quote, 'Embrace what makes you unique and special.' Sounds like your blog is nothing but a big fat lie."

Izzy frowned. "You did tell Harriet to highlight her hair, Em."

"Because she said how much she hated it and thought it was mousy!" Emma cried.

"What? You told her that her hair was mousy?" Saige interrupted. "OMG, that's so messed up!"

Emma was about to lose it. She could feel the heat rising up her neck and into her face. Everyone was attacking her—and she felt like she had no escape.

"I think dark brown hair is lovely," Jordie said, turning to Harriet. "You should have left it just the way it was. Don't ever let Emma talk you into making terrible decisions."

"Really?" Harriet seemed slightly starstruck. "You liked my hair, Jordie?"

"I mean, it was the exact same shade as Kendall Jenner's—don't you think, girls?" she asked Saige and Lyla. They both nodded enthusiastically.

Harriet turned to face Emma. "You never told me I looked like Kendall," she said. "You said I should put in blond streaks—blond like you."

"Well, there you go!" Jordie said. "She was trying to make you her little clone."

"What?" Emma shouted. "I'm not the one who wants people to follow me around—you are."

"You *are* always checking your blog to see if kids are reading it or commenting," Izzy said. "You're kind of obsessed with people following your advice."

First Saige, now her two best friends were turning against her! Emma tossed her backpack over one shoulder and ran up the steps to the front doors of the school. This was more than she could take!

Emma bolted straight up to the third-floor computer lab to take her post down. She was not going to apologize to Saige anymore. Not when Saige had completely lied about what had happened just to get a spot on the cheerleading squad. And to think, she'd actually felt bad for her! She pulled up the *Ask Emma* page and was about to delete the post when she suddenly saw something beneath it. This time, it wasn't just a comment, it was a photo with a caption—a picture of her that had been photoshopped with a giant nose and big brown polka dots on her cheeks. It read, *Keep your big nose out of other people's business!*

Emma sat staring at the screen, speechless. Who would do something like this? Jordie? Saige? Or someone who had just heard the rumors they were undoubtedly spreading and thought humiliating her would be amusing? She deleted it and quickly shut down the computer, hoping she'd gotten to it before anyone else had. She wanted to find Mr. Goddard and tell him, but the first-period bell was about to ring. She scribbled a quick note and left it on his desk: *Could we talk ASAP? Emma.*

In English class, Mrs. Cole was going over the symbolism in *The Giver* when someone in the room started laughing. Mrs. Cole gazed up from her lesson plan and saw it was not just one, but several girls who were passing around a cell phone.

"No phones in class—unless you want it confiscated for the entire week," their teacher threatened. The giggles continued the second she turned to write on the board.

"This is the funniest thing I have ever seen!" Emma heard a boy named Harrison whisper. The phone was making its way around from hand to hand under the desks. "That big nose is *genius*!"

Emma's heart started to pound. They couldn't be referring to the photo someone had posted of her, could they? She had taken it down! Maybe she was just being paranoid. Unless . . .

"Where did you get that? I thought she deleted it," someone else said.

"Screenshot. Here, I'll forward it to you."

Emma's hand went up. She suddenly felt sick to her stomach. "May I be excused, Mrs. Cole? I don't feel very well."

"I believe you've used that excuse before, Emma," Mrs. Cole told her. "There are ten minutes left in the period. You can go to the nurse after."

So Emma was stuck sitting there, trying not to pay attention to the buzz around her: the smirking, the whispering, the snide remarks. When the bell finally rang, she jumped out of her seat and raced from the room before anyone could say anything to her face. She noticed several more kids in the hall snickering as she walked by. Even Xavier was doubled over in laughter, looking at his laptop screen. She pulled him aside.

"What is it?" she asked. "Tell me."

"Um, you don't know?" he said, slightly embarrassed. "It's kind of everywhere."

"What? What's everywhere?" Emma demanded.

He opened his laptop to show her. It was an email with the subject line *You have to see this!* When he clicked to open it, the photo of her with the giant nose appeared as an attachment.

"Sorry," he said sympathetically. "You must have made someone really mad at you for them to do something like this. They emailed the entire school."

Emma checked the email address—it was from an

account she'd never heard of, not an Austen school address. There was no way of knowing who was behind this or how far it would go.

Emma saw Jordie and Saige standing at their lockers, cracking up. She wondered whether it was over the photo—and decided she needed to get to the bottom of this.

"Did you do it, Jordie?" she demanded.

Jordie batted her eyelashes. "Do what? Oh, you mean that very unflattering photo of you? Not my style—I never need to photoshop my photos. I don't even know how."

"Then it was you, Saige," Emma accused her.

"Don't go blaming me," Saige said. "Maybe it was one of your besties. They didn't seem too thrilled with you this morning."

"Harriet and Izzy would never do that!" Emma insisted. *Would they?*

"Good luck." Jordie waved her off. "Hope you find someone who 'nose' who posted that picture. Get it? 'Nose'?" She laughed in Emma's face.

Emma made a beeline for Mr. Goddard's

classroom—she had to tell him what was going on. Jackson saw her running up the stairs and chased after her.

"Emma, wait up!" he called. "I heard what's going on. What can I do?"

She paused on the second-floor landing. "You can leave me alone. You wouldn't understand."

"Try me," he said, panting from trying to catch up to her. "I'm a good listener." She realized she had told him the same thing when they first met. Then he touched her hand on the banister . . . and she crumbled.

"It isn't fair." She felt the tears tumbling down her cheeks. "I don't deserve this."

"No, you don't," Jackson said softly. "I didn't either."

Emma looked him in the eyes. "What do you mean, you didn't either?"

"You asked me why I moved from my old school," he replied. "Well, that's one of the reasons. Some kids were bullying me, so my parents moved us here, near my grandparents, so I could have a fresh start."

"You were bullied?"

"Yup. I know, someone so cool and good-looking, it's hard to believe, right?" he joked.

Emma had a sickening thought: *What if the bullying got so bad that she had to change schools and move too?* She loved her beautiful sky blue bedroom and her house with the automatic garage door that always stuck. She couldn't just pick up and leave. She couldn't let this situation get out of hand.

"Don't let them break you down. You're stronger than all of them," Jackson assured her.

She wanted to hug him for saying that but worried it might scare him off. Instead, she playfully punched him in the arm—wasn't that what guys did?

"Ow!" Jackson yelped. "I said you were strong, but you don't need to prove it. I bruise easily."

"Sorry," she apologized. "I'll be okay. And I appreciate you trusting me with your secret. It means a lot to me."

Jackson blushed, and Emma knew she'd finally

gotten to him. "Yeah, well, you seemed like you needed it," he said, ruffling his fingers through his hair.

She ran up the rest of the stairs and found Mr. Goddard at his desk. She could tell by his wrinkled brow that he knew why she was there.

"I got the email," he said, shaking his head. "Someone sent a blast to the entire school, even the teachers, from a fake account. I was able to block the address and delete it from the server, but I'm afraid it already went out to the Austen community."

"It doesn't even matter that I deleted it," Emma said. "People have taken screenshots and they're texting it around," Emma said. "Is there anything we can do?"

Mr. Goddard sighed. "I'm afraid there's not much, but I did report it to Ms. Bates immediately. She says she is asking anyone with information to step forward, and we'll be investigating it thoroughly. I promise you, we'll get to the bottom of this."

Emma shook her head. That wasn't good enough. No one would rat out the person who sent the photo or admit to taking a screenshot and spreading it around further. Trying to find the guilty party was like looking for a needle in a haystack.

"I think we should notify your parents," Mr. Goddard suggested.

"What? Why?"

"Because this is not just a prank, Emma. This is a cyberbullying incident."

"I need to do something," she told her teacher. "I need to respond somehow."

Mr. Goddard looked concerned. "I don't know if that's the best idea. Perhaps we should retire your blog until things quiet down a bit."

Emma stood up. "No. That's exactly what they want. Whoever this person or group of people is, they want me to stop giving advice." She was angry, but more than that, determined. "I want to use this to make a difference," she told Mr. Goddard. "And I know exactly how."

#

She agreed to present her idea to Mr. Goddard and Ms. Bates after school—with her mom and dad sitting in on the meeting as well. As she walked into the principal's office, she felt good knowing they were all there to support her.

"Emma, honey, are you okay?" her mom asked, hugging her. "Ms. Bates told us what happened. It's horrible!"

Emma knew how worried her parents were—but she had to convince them that she was fine and had a plan.

"Kids need to understand what this feels like, so they know it's not okay to cyberbully anyone ever again," she explained to them calmly. "I want to write a blog post about what happened to me."

Ms. Bates sat back in her chair and mulled it over. "It's a very brave thing to stand up to bullying, Emma," she said. "And I do think you could get through to a lot of kids by being so open and honest.

But are you sure you want to do this? You've been through a lot already."

Emma nodded. She felt that tingly feeling in her fingertips once more, her signal that this was the right decision. "Yes, I'm positive," she said. "I'll write it tonight. Trust me, I know what I want to say."

Her parents looked at each other, then at Mr. Goddard and Ms. Bates. They all nodded in agreement. Emma knew this was the most important post she would ever write.

CHAPTER 11

WORDS HURT

Usually Emma jumped right into writing a post, letting her fingers fly across the keyboard, struggling to keep up with her thoughts. But this post was harder. She wanted it to convey just the right tone and message. She swept her hair up into a scrunchie and changed into her comfiest pj's—the ones with the rainbow unicorns were her favorites for writing. She did some research online, then she climbed onto her bed, balanced the laptop on her knees, and closed her eyes. She let the words slowly take shape:

When you think of a bully, you think of someone who comes up to you in the schoolyard and threatens you or calls you names or hits you. You know exactly who that bully is—he or she has a name and a face. Cyberbullying is different. It can happen anywhere, anytime, on sites and apps we all use. Cyberbullies don't have to tell you who they are; anonymity is perfect for cowards. It's easier to insult a person through a screen; all it takes is a few clicks to torment and humiliate someone.

People always say words are just words and they can't hurt you—but they do. In reality, they can hurt a lot. I know this because I was cyberbullied myself. I felt hurt, angry, threatened, and alone. But then someone reminded me that I wasn't alone, and I didn't have to accept being a victim. That's the thing: none of us do.

Research shows that about 58% of kids admit someone has said mean or hurtful things to them online. They don't tell anyone; they don't try to stop it. Those are really scary statistics. It's not fair and it's not right.

Here's my advice: if you're ever bullied (I hope you never are), your first thoughts may be "What's wrong with me? What did I do wrong?" Remember: the answer is nothing. Maybe a bully lashes out because he or she feels unhappy, frustrated, even jealous. Just remember: it's not about you; it's about them. Don't respond or try to get revenge, no matter how untrue the stuff they're saying is. It won't be worth it when you turn into a bully yourself. Block them, delete them, don't let them in.

Confide in an adult you trust—your parents, a teacher, a coach, a grown-up who will listen and help you. Finally, make sure that everyone in your school knows that cyberbullying is not funny, not cool, and most important, not tolerated. Words hurt. Remember that next time you post a comment or send an email or text. There is someone on the receiving end whose life could potentially be ruined by what you say.

Emma hit Send, and it was on its way to Mr. Goddard to post on the site. She felt good about what she'd written. Somehow, writing down her thoughts, putting it out there, sharing her feelings with her peers, and asking them to take the high road, felt good. She wasn't sure what the reaction would be, if people would really think about what she'd written or just laugh it off. All she could do now was hope for the best.

The next morning, Emma climbed off the school bus and took a deep breath. Mr. Goddard had posted the blog entry bright and early in the morning and email-blasted the seventh grade about her new post, so it was a good bet that several students had already seen it. She stood there, waiting for someone to say something or react. But most of the students were either huddled in groups talking or busy on their phones. She did, however, notice Elton, seated on the bottom step, with his earphones on.

"Mozart?" she asked him.

"Actually, Chopin," he replied. "By the way, nice post."

Emma froze. "You saw it? I mean, you read it?"

"Yeah, I did. Good job." He gave her a thumbs-up.

Emma continued walking up the steps to the front door, pleased with his review. She noticed Xavier and a bunch of his track team buddies gathered at the front doors.

"Yo, Emma," he called to her. "Read your blog."

She waited for him to say anything else. Did he

like it? Did it speak to him? Had he learned something from her pouring out her heart and soul?

Xavier smiled. "FYI, nailed my last Spanish quiz. I got a ninety-one."

"Good for you," Emma replied. It wasn't quite the reaction from Xavier she was hoping for. She sat through her entire first-period class wondering whether anyone else had actually taken the time to read her blog and consider what she was trying to say. Her answer came shortly after the period bell rang.

Lyla ran up to her at her locker. "What you wrote," she said, "it was really . . . interesting."

"Uh-huh," Emma said. She was waiting for Lyla to hurl another insult at her—or call over Jordie and Saige to chime in.

"I mean, I know how you feel," Lyla said softly. "Jordie is supposed to be my friend, but sometimes she sends kind of mean texts about me to other girls on the cheer team. One time, I accidentally dropped one of my pom-poms during a game and she texted everyone that 'Loser Lyla' messed up. They think I don't know, but I do." She looked around nervously. "I've never told anyone before, but then I read your blog, and what you said you felt . . . well, I feel that way sometimes too."

Emma put a reassuring hand on her shoulder. "Lyla, you don't have to stand for that. And I'm glad you told me. We can do something about it."

Lyla's face turned pale. "No, I mean, I don't want Jordie to get mad at me. That'll just make it worse!"

"That's what a bully counts on," Emma told her. "That people will be too scared to call her out. But you should. We can go right to Ms. Bates together if you want."

Lyla shook her head. "No, I don't think that's a good idea. I changed my mind. Don't say anything. Thanks!" She ran off before Emma could try to convince her.

At lunch, both Izzy and Harriet parked their trays next to Emma's.

"Hi," Izzy said, testing the waters. "You probably hate us for doubting you—"

"We're sorry, Em," Harriet chimed in. "We should have stuck by you in front of Saige and Jordie. We know you're a good person and would never purposely do anything to hurt anyone."

"Thanks," Emma said. "I guess you read my blog."

"We did, and we feel just awful," Izzy told her. "We didn't know how bad it was. We're so, so sorry."

Emma shrugged. "It's okay. I mean, Saige did make it sound like I was the one to blame."

"But you're our BFF," Harriet insisted. "We should have stood up for you right there and then."

Emma smiled. "Well, you can do something now that's even better."

Harriet gulped. "You don't want me to go punch Jordie in the nose, do you? Because we all know I'm kind of a wimp."

Emma laughed. "No, no! No punching, no bullying. Didn't you read my blog post? Revenge is never the answer."

"Then what can we do?" Izzy asked. "Name it."

Emma dug into her backpack and pulled out a sheet of paper. On it, she'd written *Say NO to cyberbullying!* in bubble letters.

"How'd you like to help me make a few dozen of these flyers and post them all over the school—in the bathrooms, on the bulletin boards, on people's lockers. . . ?"

Harriet raised her hand like she was in class. "Just one question: Will this get us detention again?"

Emma shook her head. "Absolutely not. Ms. Bates is totally on board. In fact, she wants me to spread the message around any way I can, so kids know they can't do this to each other."

"You need a contract for this too," Harriet added. "That everyone signs and promises never to cyberbully."

Emma's eyes lit up. "Harriet, you're a genius! That's exactly what we need. And we'll get everyone to sign it, even Jordie."

"How?" Izzy asked. "I mean, Jordie is gonna want something really good in return for that. Like no PE for the rest of the school year."

"I can't promise that, but you're right—Austen Middle Schoolers will need some strong motivation." She thought it over for a few minutes as she watched Harriet poke at the cherry tomatoes in her salad bowl.

"I hate tomatoes," Harriet said, making a face. She held one up to her face. "They always remind me of a clown nose."

Izzy chuckled. "You've always hated clowns! Remember last year we went to the Holiday Festival and you freaked out a mile when one handed you a cute little balloon animal?"

"It was a balloon mouse." Harriet winced at the thought. "I hate mice more than I hate clowns."

Emma's fingertips began to tingle. "That's it!" she shouted.

Harriet and Izzy looked at each other. They had no idea what their friend was thinking—but from the look on Emma's face, it had to be something *really* good.

"I have to run and talk to Ms. Bates," Emma said,

leaving them behind at the lunch table. "I'll fill you in later—but get those flyers going!"

Izzy saluted her. "Yes, ma'am! We will be bubble-lettering all during study hall."

"Maybe even during history class," Harriet piped up. "It's soooo boring!"

Emma was excited, and for the first time in the past few days, she was really, truly happy. This was bigger than her, bigger than her blog. This was something that was going to change Austen Middle School forever!

She found Ms. Bates eating her lunch at her office desk. She knocked on her door, then barged in before the principal could even tell her to enter.

"I have a great idea," Emma said, taking a seat across from her.

Ms. Bates put down her fork. "It must be pretty great for you to burst in like this."

"Oh, it is!" Emma assured her. "You know the Holiday Festival?"

Ms. Bates nodded. "Yes, Emma, we hold it every year before winter break. Why?"

"Well, everyone looks forward to it—we

practically count the days till it's here because it's so much fun. All the games and the booths, all the holiday decorations . . ."

Ms. Bates sighed. "Thank you for the vote of approval. But you still haven't told me why you're interrupting my Taco Tuesday lunch."

"I think we can get everyone at Austen Middle School to sign a no-cyberbullying contract," Emma said.

"And how does the Holiday Festival play into that?" Ms. Bates inquired.

"That's the thing—to go to Holiday Fest, everyone has to sign it. It's the admission ticket. They have to read the contract, sign it, and pledge to never cyberbully."

Ms. Bates sat back in her chair. "That's a very interesting idea," she said.

"Is that a yes?" Emma asked anxiously.

"I'll do one better. Let's make the Holiday Festival a benefit to raise money for antibullying organizations. I'll let you pick, since you're becoming quite the expert on this subject. All ticket sales will go to the organization of your choosing."

Emma beamed—that was an even better idea! Why stop at Austen Middle School when she could actually do something to stop bullying at schools all around the country? "We can make T-shirts and stickers and buttons."

Ms. Bates chuckled. "Can I ask *Ask Emma* one more thing?"

Emma shrugged. "Sure. Shoot."

"Would you also write a blog post announcing your wonderful plan? Since everyone is now an avid reader?"

Emma raised an eyebrow. "Really? You think everyone reads my blog?"

Ms. Bates turned her computer screen to face her. There, beneath her post, were no less than eighty-five comments. Emma skimmed them:

Go, Emma! Don't let anyone dull your sparkle!

You're so right! I'm not going to let anyone put me down anymore.

Wow, this takes guts. I don't think I'd be brave enough to write this.

This is really inspiring. Thanks for sharing.

Then her eyes landed on one particular comment, which had a name attached to it:

A girl who always speaks her mind. Cool. Keep doing you. Jax

"I couldn't have said it better myself," Ms. Bates told her, reading over her shoulder. "Keep doing you, Emma. Because you are going to do great things."

After weeks of planning, it was finally the weekend of the Holiday Festival—now renamed the Say No to Cyberbullying Celebration. Everyone had volunteered to pitch in and help: Izzy and Harriet manned the giant poster board at the doors of the gymnasium, collecting five dollars from each student and handing them a Sharpie to sign the contract— along with tickets to play games.

"Read the no-cyberbullying contract carefully," Izzy instructed. "You are taking a vow to honor it."

"And Ms. Bates takes it very seriously," Harriet chimed in. "If you break the contract, it's suspension and a mark on your permanent record!"

Ms. Bates stood by the contract, arms crossed, giving her sternest of stares. She meant it!

The library, the art room, the auditorium, and several other spaces were decorated with tinsel and paper snowflakes and filled with activities, food stations, and games. Mr. Goddard had set up several computers in the cafeteria.

Elton raced over to Emma and pulled her inside. "Want a sneak peek of our science fair project?" he asked her.

"Oh, your instant-freeze ice cream?" Emma asked him.

"Well, yeah—but more fun than pouring chemicals into a beaker." He hit a button on the computer and a game popped up on the screen, "Stack up the Scoops."

"You have to pile the ice cream scoops in the bowl, and you do it by figuring out which chemical will keep it from melting," he explained. There was already a long line to play the game, and Jax was taking tickets and ushering kids to computer stations.

"It was all his idea," Elton whispered to Emma. "Jax figured since everyone is always glued to their phones and computer screens, this was a great way to get our research out there."

"Who will be the one to stack the most scoops?" Jax called to the crowd. He held up a gift card to the Ben & Jerry's in town. "The highest score gets a ten-dollar gift card for real ice cream. All it takes is a little chemistry know-how and it can be yours."

Xavier was at one computer, already punching the keys and trying to maneuver his cone so it wouldn't topple. "I'm in the lead! Twenty-six scoops and counting!" he exclaimed. "Sodium alginate as a stabilizer is the key, isn't it?" he asked Elton and Jax. "Or is it carrageenan? Or phos-pha-ti-dyl—however you pronounce it?"

"I'm not saying a word," Elton replied. "A scientist does not divulge his secrets."

Emma laughed. She'd never seen kids so excited

about chemistry. "This is brilliant! How did you come up with it?" she asked Jax. "Everyone wants to play your video game."

"Well, it was two things really," he explained. "First, who doesn't love playing video games? And second, I know this girl who writes a crazy-popular blog. She kinda gave me the idea to take our science project to the computer screen." He held up a huge bowl filled with tickets. "I bet we can raise hundreds of dollars at our booth today to fight cyberbullying. Xavier is determined to get the highest score."

Xavier handed Jax a twenty-dollar bill to play twenty games. "You bet I am! I just broke my record: thirty-one scoops and counting!"

Emma continued roaming around the booths and tables. Her dad had set up a table in the corner of the science lab, and he and Luc were handing out free squeezy stress balls shaped like hearts advertising Dr. Woods's cardiology practice.

"Did you see what we had printed on them?" her dad asked, handing her one. It read, *Have a heart! Say NO to cyberbullying!*

"Awesome!" Emma exclaimed. She saw her mom and Harriet's mom manning their own table of goodies in the hallway outside the main office. Mrs. Woods waved a double-fudge peppermint-stick brownie under Emma's nose. "Your favorite! Want one?"

Emma's mouth watered. "You bet!"

Harriet's mom held out her palm. "That'll be one dollar. We're raising money for a very important cause today. Not even the event organizer gets a freebie!"

Coach Hawkins had volunteered to take a seat in the Dunk the Teacher booth in the gym. She was already soaked from being dunked several times, but she waved at Emma happily. There was even a karaoke stage set up in the auditorium. Emma saw Jordie, Saige, and Lyla there, combing through a book of songs.

She walked over to see how Lyla was doing. They hadn't talked since the day after Emma had posted her antibullying blog post.

Lyla spotted her coming over and looked nervous. "Oh, Emma," she said. "Hey."

Jordie looked up from the song list. Emma waited for her to say something snarky, but she didn't. Instead, she went back to looking through lyrics.

It was Saige who finally spoke up. "Do you know this one?" she asked Emma. "Meghan Trainor?"

Emma couldn't believe her ears. Was Saige asking her to sing with them? Was this some kind of trick, meant to humiliate her in front of everyone? If it was, she wasn't going to take the bait. Not this time.

"No thanks, I'm kind of busy," Emma said, starting to walk away.

"We signed the contract," Jordie told her. "All of us. And we read your blog post. Lyla made us."

Lyla nodded. "I did. And they're sorry. *We're* sorry. Saige told us that maybe she did have something to do with the scarf incident."

"You told them?" Emma asked her. "Why?"

"I guess I felt bad after I read what you wrote," Saige said. "You didn't mean to mess me up at the tryouts. I was upset and kind of mean to you, and things got a little out of control."

"A *little*?" Jordie interrupted her. "You're lucky we need you to win nationals, or you would have been kicked off the cheerleading squad for lying."

Emma looked at Jordie and vaguely remembered the time way back in elementary school when they had been good friends. "Remember how we used to sing the whole soundtrack from *High School Musical*?" she asked her.

Jordie smiled ever so slightly. "I was always Sharpay, and I made you play Troy Bolton."

Emma laughed. "You did! But I never minded because I had a huge crush on Zac Efron. Still do."

"Me too!" Jordie said, forgetting herself for a moment. "Did you see he's in a new movie? I'm *so* going opening night."

"Maybe we could all go together?" Lyla suggested.

Both Jordie and Emma stopped reminiscing and stared at her.

Saige spoke up. "That would be fun. Don't you think, Jordie?" Then she pointed to a song in the catalog: "We're All in This Together" from *High School*

Musical. "I know you're in show choir, so you must be a good singer," she told Emma. "Maybe you could sing lead?"

Emma looked at Jordie to make sure she was okay with that.

"Yeah, sure," Jordie said. "As long as I get to do the Sharpay part."

They all climbed up on the stage, and when the music started, Emma belted out the first verse. Jordie joined in, with Saige and Lyla backing them up. Suddenly, a huge crowd was gathered around the stage and clapping along.

Emma took a bow and let the moment wash over her. She looked out into the audience and saw Ms. Bates, her parents, her brother, Harriet and Izzy, and right there in the front row, Jax. Everyone was cheering. Was it possible that everyone was finally coming together and treating one another with respect and kindness? Had the words she had written on her blog caused all this to happen? Yes, words could hurt, but amazingly, they could also heal.

As she climbed down from the stage, Jax came over and rested his elbow on her shoulder. "So this show-choir thing," he started, "you don't need to know how to do any skateboarding tricks to join it, do you?"

Emma giggled. "No, no ollies. You just need to be able to sing."

He scratched his head. "Yeah, I think I could do that. Did I happen to mention I played Troy in my camp production of *High School Musical*? I was seven at the time, but still . . ."

Emma's jaw dropped. "No. You didn't mention it."

He pointed to the karaoke stage. "Up for an encore?"

Out of the corner of her eye, Emma saw Izzy and Harriet jumping up and down and giving her two thumbs-up.

"Always," Emma told him.

Emma decided that her very last blog post of the semester should be something that expressed how far she had come these past few months—and how far the students of Austen Middle School had come. She curled up on the couch while her mom was cleaning up the dinner dishes, and her dad and brother were sitting down to watch a football game on TV. She opened her laptop and began to type:

We're living in a digital age, when kids are learning younger and younger how to use technology. My three-year-old cousin knows how to Google search for Disney princess pictures on my laptop, which is pretty amazing if you think about it. What it means is that we are all able to seek out information, share ideas, and communicate a lot easier than our parents or grandparents did. What it also means is that whatever you put out there in cyberspace gets seen, heard, and read, and it can create a huge reaction, whether you mean for it to or not. Kind of like the time I added vinegar to baking soda in science class. (FYI, it gets fizzy and goes everywhere—I needed a whole roll of paper towels to clean it up.)

I didn't expect my blog to take off like it has—I'm getting so many great questions from all of you and trying my best to answer at least one a day. I really appreciate that you gave me a voice at Austen Middle School and you're open to my advice. We've gotten to know and trust one another a lot more, and it's amazing that our school has pledged to wipe out cyberbullying. I know it's just one small step and we have the whole rest of the school year ahead of us. But if we can just remember what we accomplished here together, I think we'll be okay.

I originally said I'm going to try to answer a question a day. That means one more *Ask Emma* till next semester.

Sometimes you don't need a lot of words to say something important. Sometimes just a few can really sum it up. My dad is good at keeping things short, sweet, and to the point. If you ask him how his day was, he will tell you, "Fine, fine." My mom is much more of a talker. If I ask her a question, I usually get an hour-long lecture. (You see where I get it from, right?) Anyway, we had Chinese food for dinner tonight, so this seemed like the perfect question to answer:

Dear Emma,

If you had to write some words of wisdom to put in a fortune cookie, what would they be?

Signed,

Just Wondering

Dear Just,

BE BRAVE, BE KIND, BE YOU. I'LL BE HERE IF YOU NEED ME.

XO,

Emma

WHAT TO DO
IF YOU'RE BEING
BULLIED

Being bullied can feel scary, but you're not alone. Organizations like No Bully are working hard to create empathy and compassion among kids in school and online so bullying becomes a thing of the past. If, like Emma, you feel like you're being bullied, don't allow it to continue. Bullies count on your fear and silence. You can get help and you can stop the bullying cycle.

If someone posts a mean comment about you on social media . . .

Turn off the comments feature on your photos; this key prevention step helps keep you in control of your content. If you are tagged in a photo that is cruel or embarrassing, you can hide it from your profile and report it as inappropriate to the site. If the cyberbullying continues, alert your parents and your school immediately.

If you're being bullied in school . . .

Your school has the responsibility to make your campus bully-free. Speak to someone, like a counselor or teacher you trust, and ask for help. You can also try some of the following ideas.

If you feel alone . . .

Find an ally. Tell a parent, a neighbor, a relative, or a friend. Being bullied feels much worse if you try to go through this ordeal by yourself.

Start an anti-bullying campaign. Cyberbullying touches many lives, and chances are it's happening in your school or community. Talk to your principal or advisor about starting a program using No Bully's and others' resources. Education and empathy are key!

People who are repeatedly bullied may start to believe that the put-downs and insults they are receiving are actually true—don't! Changing the way that other students treat you may be difficult, but you do have control of what you think about yourself. Respect and love yourself, and positivity will follow!

Hold your head up high . . .

When you are bullied, feeling powerless is easy and that may lead you to want to give up. Don't! Stand tall and remember no one can dull your sparkle.

Call a help line. If there is no one
that you feel safe talking to, call
the Trevor Helpline immediately at
1-866-4-U-TREVOR
(1-866-488-7386).
People are there who will listen and can
understand what you're going through.
You can also text Crisis Text. For more
information, visit
https://www.crisistextline.org.

**For more advice, check out No Bully at
www.nobully.org.**

ACKNOWLEDGMENTS

This book series would not be possible without the following people. Many, many thanks to . . .

The Kahns, Berks, and Saperstones; Dad/Peter for your patience when we are "in the zone" writing and editing; Gaga Judy for studying up on *Emma*/Jane Austen and making us great curriculums and mother/daughter book club guides to share.

No Bully for empowering and inspiring us. We are so excited for your Power of Zero campaign and inspired by all that you do in and out of our schools. Thank you for letting us be a part of your courageous fight to wipe out bullying and lead us into a better world.

Jill Jaysen, your light shines so bright and inspires us every day! Thank you for all your help, faith, joy, and words of wisdom—XOXO; the kids of the Peace, Love, No Bully Movement—you have shared your voices and pledged your time and effort in so many wonderful ways. Thank you for being such great role models for your generation. Love you guys and "we're gonna make a difference . . . today!"

Rick Richter, our awesome agent at Aevitas Creative Management. Thank you for the support and cheerleading!

The gang at Bonnier Publishing USA/Yellow Jacket, led by Sonali Fry, you are all such a joy to work with! From the bottom of our hearts, we appreciate your energy, enthusiasm, and dedication to this series, and we are so proud to have Emma call Bonnier Publishing USA her home!

A *New York Times*–bestselling author several times over, **Sheryl Berk** is most proud of the dozens of books she has cowritten with her daughter, **Carrie**, including The Cupcake Club and the Fashion Academy series. *Ask Emma* is their third collaboration.

A renowned celebrity ghostwriter, Sheryl has worked with Maddie and Mackenzie Ziegler, Jack & Jack, Matthew Espinosa, Zendaya, Britney Spears, and others. Her number-one bestseller, *Soul Surfer* with Bethany Hamilton, was adapted into a major motion picture.

At only fifteen years old, **Carrie Berk** is already a bestselling children's book author, playwright, dancer, singer, actor, model, and lifestyle blogger (carrieschronicles.com). An anti-bullying crusader since elementary school, she based *Ask Emma* on her passion for blogging and her determination, as a teen ambassador for No Bully, to eradicate cyberbullying worldwide.